Scarred But Strong

Isidro Sauer

CONTENTS

PROLOGUE

It was the screaming that woke Tim up. A baby's cry that was loud and piercing. Tendra was home and with her was his nephew. Technically speaking, anyway. Tendra was more mother than sister to him. Always had been. So many times he had begged to be stronger and faster so that he could take the beatings she got. So many times he had pleaded with her to hide with him under his bed and still she told him to go and leave her. And like a coward he had hated his pathetic self for seven years.

He had been weak. He had been vulnerable and his weakness had led to his sister taking pain; the pain he was too childish to handle. Then Ray came along and saved Tendra, and Tim had been both grateful and disheartened. He had wanted to save his sister but he hadn't managed it. Now he felt he owed everything to Ray. Ray told him he wasn't a coward. He knew it to be otherwise.

Now though he had a second chance. Tendra had fallen pregnant with her mate's child. A baby boy they had proudly announced to the pack and now the child was at the bottom of the stairs. Tim was up, running towards his bedroom and wrenching it open. He smiled with joy, Tendra was beaming though dark shadows under eyes told him she was tired. In her arms was what looked like a bundle of white woollen blankets that the pack had made for her. But the closer Tim got, as he descended the stairs, the more he could see that there was a peachy coloured skin underneath. That and there was also a terribly persistent noise coming from it.

"Let's see Tendra." He begged and Tendra knelt down so he had a better view of the tiny baby in her arms. The large round blue eyes turned from Tendra's face to Tim's curious one and he was met with an acceptance that overwhelmed him. The tiny child stopped crying and started waving its arms around. Tim wasted no time in catching, in his hand, one of the baby's and he watched with fascination as the little fingers curled around his index finger with a strength that took him by surprise for one so small. The cute wrinkled skin of the baby fingers wound tight around him, stopping him from moving and keeping him standing - captivated by the new member of his family.

He knew in that moment that this was his chance to do for someone else what Tendra had done for him. Protect. He would watch over his nephew with a vigilance that would upstage every other warrior of the pack. He would allow his nephew to have the freedom and happiness in life that had been denied to Tim for seven years of his existence. And Tim would make sure his nephew never had to go through any of the pain that he and his sister had had to bear so many times in their past.

Tim looked expectantly up at Tendra who knew instantly what he wanted. "His name is Christopher." She told him with pride in her voice. Taking his eyes away from his sister he knew he had to be quick, Ray was moving from behind her to no doubt send everyone back to bed and take Tendra to their room, so she could rest herself. Looking back at his nephew Tim made every last second count. He lent over and kissed the hand that gripped his finger and murmured into the baby's ear. "I will always be there for you Christopher. Always."

Tim stood on the edge of the forest with his back to the pack house which Tendra was calling him from. He had finished school only that day and Tendra was trying to hold a celebration for him but he kept telling her that he didn't want one. The weekend was supposed to be full of food, dancing and lots of proud adults talking about their children growing up before their very eyes. Tim was looking at his Thursday with a different outlook.

School had been difficult for him. Not the academics, that had been too easy. He had been forced year after year to attend class and do homework for subjects he had been studying at university level at for years out of school time. He told them that he needed harder work, that he knew the answers but they laughed at him. So he passed every subject with an A star grade. The highest grade passes and the monotony of school had made it so that as Tendra went on and on about college and university he remained quiet, knowing he wasn't going to either.

What had been particularly difficult had been socialising. The boys that were his age in years were not his age in mind. He had seen too much, suffered through too much and finally achieved his wolf self at the age of seven - almost nine years too early. He did not play 'games' like they did. Their make believe land was too boring and unimaginative to him. Football was not a game to him; the boys in his classes only saw a pitch and a ball. Tim saw a battle field which his analytical mind tried to win using tactics and pre planning and a lot of assessing. The running the children did was barley a stretch in the legs for Tim. Games lesson were a stroll in the park compared to the challenges to his class. They both admired his 'cool' and 'mature' demeanour while at the same time were jealous and soon excluded him from their 'normal' games.

The hardest thing of all though, growing up, was not the schooling, nor the children he was forced to be amongst but the adults around him. The adults who knew what he had been through, knew his transformation into a mature wolf and had once knelt to him, now shunned and pushed him away. By his tenth birthday he had been doing weight training and running laps of the territory before school. He was physically capable of being a warrior and had the mind frame for it; having been in battle himself before. Yet when he asked to join them they laughed at him.

The patronising pat on the shoulder when they told him to train for a few more years and come back when he was sixteen was hard to hear. He showed them year after year every single birthday from his tenth that he was physically capable. He took part in tactical challenges and puzzles once every year to prove to them he was good enough. By his thirteen birthday they finally let him fight a warrior, Tim was evenly matched and he knew it, he fought the fight but tripped at one point. He was eyeing up his recovery even as the ground got closer but the warriors called off the match told Tim he had lost. They refused every year after to let him fight. He had not lost, his backside had not even touched the ground. They did not let him be a warrior and he was not even allowed to train with them.

Tendra made every single meal. He loved how she was good at that, how every Thursday she made one of his favourite dishes and as he got older he knew that Wednesday was Christopher's favourite dish day and Thursday was his. He secretly wanted to cook a meal for her in thanks but the kitchen was her domain. She liked to cook. Christopher was growing up pampered and full of joy. He asked Tim to play with him and Tim did. He could ask anything of Tim and as a devoted uncle Tim gave him everything he asked for, unless it broke one of Tendra's rules.

But all in all, after everything he had lived through, this, standing with his back to the pack was the hardest thing in the world. To stand there knowing Christopher was at the door waiting for him to get home and Tendra was still shouting him for dinner was hard.

"Tim, your sister is shouting, surely you can hear her from here." Tim whipped around to see Lewis stood there. His best friend. The only friend he had that had stuck by him through thick and thin and told Tim to be who he was and not let the kids get on his nerves. Lewis had seen some terrible things in his life as well but he didn't talk about them. That was the silent rule between them, no talking about the day Lewis was found or of any day before that. Tim obliged, his own past was off limits to questioning. His shame ran deep.

"I hear her."

"Then are you coming to dinner?"

Such a simple question. That Tim answered with his own.

"Heard any more news about the pack moving in from the east?"

"Not that I have heard or seen."

"The information is getting harder and harder to gain."

"Or maybe the warriors have just figured out we are snooping around."

"They would have told Tendra and I would definitely know about it. The pack is getting better, this wayward pack."

"There is nothing we can do Tim."

"They are getting closer to us."

"And Ray knows it and will sort it out. This is allied territory, we have many packs here. We will be fine."

"You can't be sure of that." Always on guard, always prepared, never complacent. That was Tim's living motto.

An awkward silence followed and Lewis walked closer, Tim could not only hear the light footfalls but he sensed the creeping of his best friend. The hairs on his back were slowly starting to stand to attention. Lewis was not a threat but the sensory instincts of his wolf were always on edge, always prepared. It was something he couldn't help but find incredibly useful. It was just something he didn't tell his friends or family about for fear of offending them.

"Come on Tim, come and eat, the alpha's will take good care of the packs that why we have them and besides Christopher is wondering where you are."

Tim turned around from facing the trees all around. Their greenery had never felt so suffocating and yet held an air of liberation. He had stared at their contradiction for about an hour and he was slowly starting to see what he needed and wanted to do.

"Lewis, have they sent a patrol guard to the lake yet?"

"What? No, usual guards are out. Nothing different."

Tim sighed, he knew what he needed to do. What he had to do. And he wondered how much was selfishly for himself and how much wasn't. He followed Lewis back towards the pack, his friend's eyebrows were frowning, uncertain and confused at Tim's behaviour; trying to work him out. He stopped when he could see Christopher bobbing up and down, getting ready to prattle on about his day with the young pups while Tendra was stood at the door waiting to greet him.

The world looked so content. Tendra looked so happy. There was a time when he could never have imagined that carefree happiness on her face. He thought he would forever have to see the forced smiles that she put on just for him. She still had on a flowery apron and Tim stopped dead in his tracks when Ray joined her and looked proudly towards him. He was not someone to be proud of. He had known that when he let Tendra take the beatings for him, he knew it now when he was going to shatter their dreams. He wasn't going to college and he would never step foot inside a university.

Lewis stopped at the side of him and Tim found himself putting hand on his only friend's shoulder. "You've been such a good friend. I'm sorry. To you... and to them." He couldn't take a another step. He couldn't make himself walk inside the claustrophobic house and greet pack members. He couldn't go back and live a life of false pretence, of knowing he was an adult and being raised as a child. He couldn't go back to being denied the ability to grow, to learn, and to be who he was. He couldn't go in there and disappoint everyone and he couldn't take the rejection another year. His sixteenth birthday was in two weeks and he knew the warriors would once again laugh at him instead of letting him join their ranks.

Christopher's smile faded, it was as if the child understood what no one else did in that first few seconds. Christopher understood and his face fell, his eyes went dull and the shine was lost but Tim knew he was young enough to get back the laughter and joy. He still hated to do this. He promised his nephew he would always look after him, be there and protect him and while that would never change the pack he lived with wouldn't let him do it. They didn't see what Tim saw. They underestimated him and now at the lake there was a dead wolf, courtesy of Tim because that wolf had been spying on their pack. A threat had got within shouting distance to the children and no one but Tim knew.

He had saved the pack but two hours earlier and he vowed to carry on doing so every day of his life. But they would never know. He took a pace back and watched as a frown formed on Tendra's face. Lewis turned abruptly and threw out a hand to stop him but no one could match Tim. He was gone another five paces backwards in the blink of an eye thanks to his wolf. Ray out the door in a second and one simple wolf cough had the other allied alpha's there along with five warriors. So this would be a chase. Tim didn't think leaving a pack would be quite that easy but he had hoped his family wouldn't try to impose ruthless alpha commands on him.

His decision was made however, he was no longer part of this oppressive pack. He was done being a coward and being shunned. He was tired of living in a façade. So he began running and as soon as he heard the heavy footfalls of wolves behind he turned and offered them a sad smile. His eyes glistened a little but he had not cried since he was seven years old and he would not cry now. "I'm sorry. Goodbye."

He ran.

They followed and yet in wolf form they still could not keep up with his human figure though they were very close. He felt the air on his ankles when a wolf almost caught him but a leap in the air had taken him out of the danger zone by the skin of his teeth. How they would now regret underestimating him. The border was half a mile away so he carried on sprinting. He refused to change into his wolf form simply because he knew he had no need to. The border was three leaps away. He did not look back instead he leapt thrice and cleared the territory.

He heard that they had come to a stop.

"Tim!" Ray called after him, authority and confusion deep in his growl.

"You too late." Tim called back without stopping or looking at him. "Check the lake." He gave them their last warning.

CHAPTER 1

A rustle to the left caught his attention. It was ever so slight. A mere insect movement in the midst of a forest but it caught his attention. Nothing should be moving. There was something lurking in that bush which all wildlife around could sense, as could he; the danger was very close to hand. Wildlife, insect or not did not move when such a threat was upon them. Which meant that the very slight whisper of movement was no insect; it was whoever dared to try and bring down the pack Tim he was watching over.

The sun had started to fade a long while ago and all that was left was a dim glow blurring his left hand side peripheral vision slightly. As little as his vision was actually impaired it was enough that he was frustrated over it. His eyes were narrowed looking to the far side of where he was standing. The sound of children playing far off was only a reminder of what was stake should he fail. The threat smelt funny, it had a sickeningly sweet pungent smell almost like decaying fruit. It was distant, faint, meaning it belonged to something that had left, and left quickly but it was getting stronger and he knew it was sneaking up behind him having left only to circle back on him in the hopes of attacking.

His ears were pulled back a little, listening to everything and taking it all in. The children, the adult voices, the footsteps of guards changing shifts, the retreat of footsteps signalling the tired guards that were making their way back to their homes. They would be less alert, easily caught and as fatigued as they would be from a long day's work, their initial struggles would not be as strong as someone at full strength. Tim knew that and paid particular attention their progress home.

The ground was on a very, very slight incline, so slight it would not really be much of an advantage but he was able to use it as such. Feeling the slight cool air that waved over the back of his neck he could feel that it was too strong to be caused by the summer's dusk weather. It was the sign that someone was right behind him, about to strike at him. But he was agile.

Whipping around he flung up an arm to feel something strike his forearm; the loud clap sound of the impact told Tim he should have felt pain from that move but he was concentrating too much on his follow through attack to be thinking of the pain. Ignoring that he threw up his other arm and with his lengthened fingernails let his claws slash at the face infront of him. It was a furred face and not one from the pack that Tim was protecting. The wayward pack that had decided to try and take over the wolves of the entire area had decided to send this highly skilled, but not quite Tim's match, to try and bring down another pack. And in wolf form as well.

Unperturbed Tim dragged down his claws cutting four stripes into the snarling face then using that very slight incline of the ground as leverage to use for extra power. Using the balls of his feet to push off from the ground he launched at his attacker, bringing down the animals and wasting no time in wrapping his hands around the animal's neck. It snarled loudly.

"Do you want the guards to come for you, you missed the last shift, newer and fresher guards are now running the perimeters." Tim taunted the powerful wolf underneath him, it snarled again this time quieter but no less annoyed.

"Don't be annoyed, you should have known this pack would not be so easy to bring down. They are under my protection." A chortling cough sort of noise forced Tim to squeeze his hands further around the wolf neck and snarl with his own wolf mutated throat. "You do not touch those I protect. You have made an enemy tonight; one you can not afford to have." The wolf under him laughed again and Tim decided to up the pressure.

He knelt on the belly of the wolf so all his weight was pin pointed on that one knee so the wolf under him was supporting a fully grown and muscle pumped man on one small spot. The discomfort to the wolf was enough to gain Tim his whole attention. "Glad you're now listening to me." The wolf snarled, Tim punched it. "Leave, crawl away on your belly, it is the only warning I will give to you. You attack again and I will kill you. I am merciful amongst many other traits not quite so honourable. Not many others will warn you, nor will they have the ability to kill you. I do both. Leave and never return. I assure you I am far from this kind when disobeyed."

He got back to his feet swiftly. He had made sure to build his muscles to such a level that he was powerful yet not enough to impair his agility and flexibility. He worked hard on keeping his body at just the right level for optimum fighting skill. Rising he cast back one hard look - just to prove his point - then he turned his back and was about to walk back to his spot when he felt again that give away breeze. Not only that but he heard the tiny tap of the foot pushing harder off the ground; harder than normal to reach further despite being on the wrong side of an incline. The wolf had lunged forward and while Tim heard it the sting on his side was enough to tell him that the wolf had cut him with his claws. Tim was already in the motion of a kick however so the wolf was soon brought again down to his back. Tim wasted no time in kneeling down besides the snapping wolf and wrapping an hand once more around its neck. "You disobeyed."

The wolf made for a fatal attack, a snap towards Tim's throat but Tim simply squeezed his hand at the same time as punching the muzzle. The punch knocked the wolf into a dazed state and in that time Tim managed to strangle the wolf until it was riding on unconsciousness. Tim made sure the wolf when from unconscious to dead.

Standing back up Tim looked at himself. Four long scratches ran down his side and though he was starting to heal he had bled a little. His arm looked fine but for tiny shrapnel marks from where his arm had originally blocked the wolf's attack it's teeth had broken his skin in some places. He shook his head at the kill infront of him; he still wasn't proud of his kills but he knew them to be necessary, no one else gave a warning but that was his thing. That was his mercy and it was a rare one at that in the wolf world but he always warned them. He gave them a chance to walk away and never look back. He gave them a chance to save their lives but they never took it.

He would leave the wolf out in the open at that exact spot to be found and show the Alpha that his pack was in danger, that it was being observed and maybe the guards would up their game. Thing that was incredible was that it was not just one pack here. It was allied with three other packs. Tim glanced back once more at the trees that blocked his full view of the clearing where the children could be heard and seen playing games. Caught sight of a young boy in a yellow shirt and a grown teen in blue chasing him Tim bowed his head. He came here every day and yet the sadness never left him. He was forced every day to do what he had eleven years ago. He turned his back on his old pack, "Goodbye Christopher." He whispered to the blue shirted teen. Leaving his brother had never gotten easier.

The trip back to his cabin was a long one, he lived so far away now; in the deep of the forest he hid out his days in seclusion. He worked part time at a human car garage fixing cars. He had left his pack and got an apprenticeship as a mechanic; three years later he was a fully qualified mechanic and worked part time. He enjoyed his work and he was around so many people he picked up on human gossip. He had found that some of it turned out to be crucial to his own full time work.

Disappearances of humans and the strange goings on gave him clues to the pack that was moving in and trying to surround the entire county and take over all packs in that distance. Tim wondered if other counties within the country had also been targeted but getting that information was harder, he needed to travel in order to get that information but he wasn't able to with his dedication to Tendra and the pack. Not to mention he was running patrol for as much area as he could, taking in rogues and advising them where to go that was safe from attack that he knew of. To top it off he had commitments to those rogues who had asked for his protection, choosing instead to remain in the area close to him instead of seeking another pack to join. In general though information was hard to get and only getting more scarce as this strange powerful pack was taking over so easily.

He opened the door to his cabin and touched the frame before he entered. It was now a ritual of his. It reminded him of the hard work he had done for three weeks in cutting down, shaping and sanding trees before building his very own home. He had loved every minute; his fifteen year old self had relished in the physical activity and end accomplishment.

Going inside he stripped from his clothes and washed up in a bucket of cold water, that he had brought in that morning from the stream, to combat the heat of the day that had him sweating. Naked he went to his ground floor room where he had weights and bars and began his work out. He enjoyed the activity, it was a way to exercise his restless wolf and his wolf was always restless it seemed. He hadn't expected his eighteenth birthday to be much of a change, in fact he almost forgot it in his self imposed isolation, but his wolf didn't. The wolf had put him on edge and the slightest thing would set him bursting his clothes and running through the forest on four legs with a lot of fur. He had called in sick to his boss when he realised he had no control and he still remembered that two weeks of hell.

At that time he had sat naked on the cold December grass and let the cold bite at his skin. His wolf had raged at him, told him to run and he internally shouted back at the beast and told him that he had two weeks to learn control. Two weeks of strict meditation, furious exercise and constant cold showers under the waterfall had taught Tim a strict discipline of self control he no longer wavered from. That didn't mean his wolf didn't let him feel that edge and restlessness though; it just meant Tim didn't give in to the instincts. But now he was a grown man, fully in control of his wolf and himself and he remembered this each time he finished a work out and felt at peace.

Tim began to cut up the carrots and boiled rice in a pan over his make shift stove. He had built it himself and lit a fire every morning to use for boiling water and cooking his food. He hadn't any contacts nor means to hook his secluded cabin up to electricity and water so he lived wild. He loved it on most days; it gave him something to do to overcome the silence that bothered him. It made his life harder and he liked the physical challenge and the constant working. If he was working he was distracted from the guilt and shame and loneliness that ate at him every second of the day.

He hunted regularly, his wolf needed it and Tim used it as a means of bringing back food to prepare for his human side. He usually ate rabbits and fish. His diet was basic; the money he earned from his part time mechanics job bought his rice and the few vegetables that he didn't grow in his back yard. Carrots, potatoes and apples were his favourite to grow though every year he changed the mix.

The meat he had caught yesterday and salted to keep for today he now cooked and put with the rice and vegetables before dishing it up on a plate and sitting down to eat it. He had no television, no radio, a few books scattered his little ground floor cabin but as for entertainment he had very little of it. He had got used to living alone, in the middle of a forest with strange noises of wildlife and insects all around him. He wasn't scared like he used to be, he knew now what was normal and what wasn't. He knew when things were amiss around him and when he was perfectly safe. Tonight he was perfectly safe. So he lay in bed and closed his eyes hoping Ray, the alpha of his old pack, had found the dead wolf and stepped up his security.

CHAPTER 2

T he waterfall was beating down on the back of his neck and shoulders, the powerful rush of water kneading his muscles and straightening out the knots they had gotten themselves into. The cold water felt good on his heated skin. He had woken up that morning and done a workout, a hard workout, and then gone for a run trailing all over the forest looking for danger. The sweat had long since been washed away with the waterfall but he was due in work in an hour and he knew he had to leave shortly and get ready.

He was only in for four hours today, he liked this shift; it was short and started late which meant he had been able to spend the morning running over what he affectionately thought of as 'his land'. Though he did share it often. The cooling foam bubbling around his waist were the water came up to when he stood on a particular rock. It was a deep pool but the current was strong, he used wolf strength to maintain his balance on the rock so as to not get swept away. The water crashing from the rocks above him was so powerful it would be hard for a human to remain there without getting dragged under. He loved his wolf self. He cherished every moment of its existence. For years he had cried out to be stronger and now he was he relished in the things he was able to do.

The fish around him were swimming away, acting as though the current was slow and graceful as they slapped their tails side to side and glided underneath the water. He sometimes wished that his life could be as calm as that but in the end he did like the challenges life gave him. He thought he might get bored if suddenly there was nothing to do. Scrubbing at his hair one last time to get out the soap he finally swam away from the waterfall and after making sure no one was around, pulled himself out of the water. His naked body rippled with muscle yet he was lithe and graceful in his own powerful way. He was crouched on the ground, knees bent and fingertips maintaining his low position. He smelt something off.

Casting his head upward he sniffed breathing in the air around him. There was no threat and it wasn't the sickly sweet pungent smell of the wayward pack. He was not being taken over or attacked but the smell was one he definitely didn't recognise. Hurriedly standing he took a step in its direction - it must be a rogue. Judging by the smell it was a wounded and terrified wolf. The smell of fear was strong in his nostrils. Wasting no time he took off at once.

Bursting into his wolf form he padded across the land, crushing the blades of grass under his weight and stepping on twigs and small thin branches that made up the forest. The undergrowth was springy in many areas where there were no paths. He let his paws sink into the green moss and flowers and dirt as he went to the aid of yet another rogue out alone in the dangerous world.

The ground rose and he started to let the muscles in his legs surge him forward in a springing leap rather that his usual running. For some reason today he was more alert and felt the necessity of getting there exceptionally quick. He had always tried to get to the rogues as fast he could but today he felt like he had to be even faster than usual. With his wolf eyes open wide, taking in every single flower petal and tree that surrounded him, he searched for a wolf. But found none.

Coming to a halt he moved in a slow circle trying to pin point the smell and locate it. He searched the ground twice over and still could see no sign of a wolf. The scent was close though, so very close it tickled at his nose in a tantalising caressing way. Then he understood his mistake, the rogue was not on the ground. He cast his eyes upwards and felt his heart stop. Draped over two thick branches was the body of a woman. A woman dressed all in white, the material was wrapped around her body, draping elegantly over her curves and tiny body, but ripped in places. The woman must have wrapped it around her to stop it catching on the branches and splinters of the tree while she climbed.

Her body was limp, the bow of her back supported by the branches and her head lolling back. It looked beautiful but the reality of it was that she had most likely gone up the tree to hide and look out for danger but in her weakness had fainted. As any adept wolf would have done she had sat in a position that meant if she fainted she would not fall to the ground; hence two branches holding her up the way his arms would if he was carrying her bridal style.

He wasted no time in letting his body change back to its human form while completely forgetting that he was naked and she a scared woman. Still he reached up and let his rough and calloused hands grip the branches and pull him upward until he was level with her. Her face was white, too white and her eyes were closed. He took a little comfort in her lips being red it meant she wasn't dead but his heart was still beating loudly at the thought of her injured. Holding onto the trunk of the tree with his strong legs he reached one of his arms out. His arm looking rather thick in comparison to hers it was a stark contrast of how masculine his body was in relation to her delicate and petite frame. He felt his mouth go a little dry as he took on her body. Her cinched in waist accentuated her breasts and the curve of her hips and thighs nicely.

Swallowing he shook his head, he couldn't be thinking of an injured wolf like this so wrapping a hand carefully around her waist he pulled her further towards the trunk so he could reach her with both hands. He took hold of her body and glanced, again, at her face. Her eyes were still closed which made his worry because she hadn't woken at his touch. It meant she needed medical attention immediately. He could smell blood on her but it wasn't a lot. He expected she was exhausted more than anything. Placing her over his shoulder he began to the climb back down. It was half way down that her body lurched and scream filled his ear but he should have realised that putting her upside down while he climbed was not the best way for her wake up.

Her nails dug into his waist and he found that the pain of her claws was thrilling rather than painful. The need to readjust his pants became a little insistent but thankfully he managed to cling on to the tree. He knew had to ignore his own desires and start calming down the frightened wolf.

"It's ok; I'm not going to hurt you. I've got hold of you but I need to get you down from the tree." Her screaming stopped but she started to shake instead. Once safely down to the ground he began to right her body but didn't let go

Setting her down he stared at her for a minute expecting her to blurt out questions or start to cry or something of the sort but she didn't. She stared at him right back, right in the eye and while they were wide and she swallowed more than normal in her fear it was clear she wasn't going to be talking anytime soon. For a while he just looked at her back while feeling a snarl of desire rumbling at the back of his throat; he wanted to be physically closer to her than he was. He had deliberately left at least five steps between them for her benefit but now he wanted to close that gap. When she took a step back from him however he knew there was no chance of getting that close that quick.

"I'm really not going to hurt you." He reassured. "I get a lot of rogues in this area but it's dangerous. There's a pack trying to take all the packs in this county."

"A county is large area they can not take it all."

"They're currently doing a good job of it." He told her dryly. "Listen, you can stay with me tonight or I can take you straight to the waterfall. There are a lot of rogues who have gathered there for a while. I initially took them there to hide but some didn't want to leave, especially since the waterfall is part of my protection. You are welcome to go there, you will be safe there until you need or want to move on. But you can not stay here."

A look in her eye caught him off guard. "I want to stay here, alone." She was testing him, he sensed it only when he felt his wolf instinct jumping painfully inside of him and he involuntarily let out a growl of anger and a command that she do as he said. It even surprised him he had lost control enough to growl.

"I'm so sorry, I don't know what has come over me. I have never been so rude before. Forgive me, I thought only of your safety."

"You're like that because we are mates."

That look in her eye disappeared. That need to test faded as she confirmed in her own mind what eluded Tim. She bowed her head - she now belonged to a man and she wasn't so sure how she felt about that. It would be nice to be able to relay on someone and know they would always be there for her but she had never thought she would meet her mate or that he would be a rogue. Rogues had no pack, they were always in danger and there was a chance he was dangerous for her to be with anyway, not much good came from being rogue, or mating to one. Her apprehension must have shown because he took a step closer to her and held out a hand. She had been through and seen too much in the last few days for such a gesture though and she flinched backwards from him.

Tim had thought that the day he left his pack was the day he also gave up with the idea of a mate. As a rogue living life looking after others from the shadows he had never thought he would meet a mate, or that he would be able to provide for one. He felt awfully embarrassed now at his makeshift hut and lack of modern appliances that would give her an easy life. He thought of how he cooked his food and even boiled the water and how he washed in the cold waterfall. That wasn't the life a lady should live. He couldn't take his eyes from though, her beauty was literally stunning him. It took a few minutes but Tim finally understand that he was in shock at finally finding his mate. He was speechless.

She had flinched at his outstretched hand but that was ok, he could be patient.

"You are hurt, I have a cabin, it's my home, small but ok. Anyway," He cursed his rambling and tried again, "Come with me and I will see you safely through the night and take you to the rogues tomorrow."

"Take me to the rogues?" Her voice sounded incredulous - he was going to hand her over to the dangerous part of society?

"They are honourable. They run from threats they are not a threat in themselves. Do not fear them. Some have become good friends of mine." He smiled at her. As much as she found herself staring at his mouth and his white teeth she already heard it in his voice. That arrogance that she should trust what he trusted in. All males had it and it made her frown. Her sides was hurting her though and she was very tired. Hungry to but she wouldn't tell that to this stranger. She had a little pride left and if it was between sleeping in trees out in the open, exposed to anyone that might come to her, or to go with her mate she would take her mate. It was the safer option; there less chance of getting hurt with this man, mates didn't hurt each other.

Still ignoring his hand she took a little step in his direction and encouraged he started walking her back.

"So what brings you out here, alone and injured."

"Don't want to talk about it."

Tim looked back at her, she was following behind him, looked begruntled and unamused but the tiny spark in her eye of sadness not only made his heart twinge. He couldn't image how she was feeling at that moment, her steps were shaky, she looked exhausted and he expected her to fall at any minute. So he slowed his pace down and hovered by her side. She said nothing.

When he had been running to find her he hadn't realised just how far from his cabin he had ran. Now he noticed it was far too long away for her to manage. "Let me help you."

"I can manage."

"No you can't. Please. I swear to you I won't do anything to you." She knew she shouldn't trust a stranger but this was her mate and the more he looked at her with that friendly eye the more she wanted to let him help her. Hell she needed the help she was tired she felt like she might fall asleep even as she walked.

For the third time that day he held out his hand to her and she pondered taking hold of it. Taking a deep breath she held out her own and let him help her. He wound an arm around her waist and kept hold of her hand helping her walk by taking most of her weight. She managed to go another ten minutes before her legs gave out.

She expected him to lower her to the floor, for his support to be only a little aid to stop her crashing completely but she was pleasantly surprised when instead of falling she was gathering into strong arms and carried.

"Thank you." She muttered as her eyes started to close. His chest rose and fell with the rhythm of his breathing and it soothed her. Resting her head on his chest its soft movements lulled her further into sleep until she drifted off. Tim looked down at the woman in his arms: his very own mate!

CHAPTER 3

Tim never thought he would have any woman in his home. Rogues were generally men and his guest room had had many males sleeping there when they needed a place to stay for the night and warm food and information. But the visits had been fleeting; he had seen a rogue to the safety of his waterfall and given them information on how to pass through the land unnoticed. They had either used that information and gone or they had stayed there and allowed him to protect them. His guest room was scarcely decorated and never before had a woman stayed in his home. He had seen only two women in all his time here and he had taken them straight to the waterfall. Women needed a lot more reassurance than males did for the simple reason that they were not as strong. They feared Tim and thought that if he hurt them they would not be able to defend themselves against him. Males told themselves they could fight Tim if he turned out to wrong them. Not that Tim would do that but he admired the male pride sometimes. He knew many of them would last less than a minute in a fight with him but they shrugged it off none the less, feigning confidence. Tim had purposely trained his body to a warrior with no equal.

After everything he had given up to be a warrior he had not let isolation get to him. He had pushed himself so hard that he made sure the leaving of his family would never be in vain. It was not his pride that told him could win the battles; it was desperate training that shaped him into a killer with few equals.

Looking around at his home he felt it inadequate to bring his mate back to but it was all he had so he carried her in through the door and towards his guest bedroom on the second level. He had figured out how to build an upstairs with supports and he was pleased to say it was sturdy though he purposely did weight training downstairs - he wasn't silly enough to actually tempt his first building that much. The room had a single bed and unfortunately only one chest of drawers and plain white pain on the walls. The drawers themselves were ones had built himself.

Removing her shoes and sliding her in the bed he let her sleep. He had to keep an eye on her though the smell of blood while not life threatening was strong. That would have to be tended to when she woke up. In the meantime he left her and started to prepare a broth and bread for her. By the stove he felt his happiness dull a little more. Tendra would never get to see his mate, a happy family reunion wasn't miraculously going to happen and there would be no family meal at festive moments of the year. In short he was bringing his mate into a life of isolation and stark quietness. The more he pondered on that the more he felt shame for running away all those years ago, he would most likely never accepted back. It was his own fault and he had come to terms with his stupidity a long time ago but now at this turning point of his life, when he had a mate and he wanted to buy a bottle of champagne and share it with his friends and family, he was reminded that he had no one to share such happiness with.

So he vowed he would buy himself and his beautiful mate a bottle to share between them. He would go to the waterfall as was his usual patrol and he would tell all his acquaintances. He didn't think they would call him a friend, he protected them but he very rarely conversed with him and he didn't stay for meal and such like even when they offered but they were the only ones he could share his happiness with. They would be happy for him, it was a fine thing for everyone when one found their mate.

He cursed; he had missed his shift at work. So caught up in his new mate he forgotten that he was supposed to be at work. Sighing he took out his mobile, the only luxury he had in his wild life, and he quickly dialled his boss.

"I'm so sorry." He said, "Something's happened. I found a woman unconscious and I had to help her, I won't be able to make it in today. I tried but I can't, sorry." He barley gave his boss a chance to speak so desperate to explain and keep his job.

"Well Tim, I can't really argue with you if you're going to play hero and help out a lady now can I? In future a head's up would be nice but I figured when you were an hour late that you wouldn't be in today. I've already got you're shift covered, you owe Hunter for that by the way. You're on a personal day."

"Thanks Terry, it's appreciated."

"I'm only being nice because this is the first time. I do have a reputation to hold though so next time I'll be angry."

"Yes boss."

He went back to check on her but she didn't seem to be stirring anytime soon so he got hold of his largest pot and made his way back to the waterfall. He need to bring back water to boil for his mate. He really needed to find out her name.

"Tim!" A shout from below him called out. Tim looked down from the rocks he was walking along. Underneath him was a well hidden rock formation that layered down further into the earth, the waterfall was just a little to his left. A beautiful river behind him flowed to the end of the rocks and as they stopped abruptly the water had a thirty foot drop. An adept rock climber or a wolf with acute skills could climb down following the gushing water that carried on flowing along another river channel at the bottom. The rocks circled the waterfall on three sides and gave way to once more to the forest on all sides. It was indeed a wonderful place to visit for the calm and tranquillity it offered. Tim however sent his men here because of the water source and hiding places.

With large boulder sized rocks creating disk shaped perches and rocks that jutted out on many levels it was inevitably filled with nooks that one could hide behind. Small man sized holes littered the surroundings while offering a wide view of everything else. The sound of the water crashing to the river was loud, it covered the sound of people scurrying to hide. The downside to that was that it masked the sound of danger approaching but with good look-out guards that could easily be combatted. The men that lived here had had to learn to live as wild as Tim. He looked down at Lauri who was wearing only a pair of shorts.

"You running the usual patrol?" He called to Tim.

"No, I'm here for water."

"I thought you were supposed to be at work."

"I found my mate." He called down.

For a minute there was just silence and then slowly, emerging from the rocks from behind and underneath came the scurrying of many people. They emerged into the summer's day and stood underneath Tim looking up at him in silent awe.

"Well I know I wasn't expecting it either but your shock isn't doing my self-esteem any favours." He said chuckling.

"Sorry Tim, we're so pleased for you. You need to bring your ladyfriend along and we can all celebrate together. In fact; tonight. Bring her tonight, we'll sort the food out. It'll be good to see another female."

"My mate is injured and exhausted. I don't know where she's come from and she's sleeping at the moment. If she is well enough and wants to then I'll bring her tonight but I need to make sure she is well enough first."

"The food can keep until tomorrow if you can't come tonight."

"Thank Lauri. Morning all." He nodded to all the people and made his way over to the waterfall that wasn't so far away.

"Wait!" He heard behind him. Turning he saw a young boy hurrying to climb the rocks, his excitement at reaching Tim was making his moves slopping and in worry for the lads safety Tim rushed over and grabbed his arm.

"You need to be careful climbing these rocks, they hide under the water as well and if you were to fall there's no telling if you would survive the fall into the water." He cautioned the young one. It was a teenager on closer look. Brendon if he remembered correctly.

"Brendon?"

"Yeah, that's me." The boy practically beamed. "Why don't you stay and have lunch with us? We have the food already prepared and all you would have to do is grab a plate and eat with us."

"I'm sorry Brendon but my mate is injured and I must care for her." The words sounded delicious in his mouth, he felt the sides of his lips moving upwards as he relished the word 'mate.' The boy however looked downhearted. "How about though you stay with me while I fill my pot up? My mate needs clean water."

"Ok. I'll go ahead and wrap you and your mate some food up." The boys smile was back on his face and he started to wind his way down the rocks looking rather skilled in the journey. Brendon wasted no time looking for foot holes and places to hold onto as he lowered his body; it was as if he had done the journey many times. And Tim had to remind himself that he having lived here for years the teen no doubt had. Tim himself climbed down the rocks at least once a week to wash under the waterfall, but he spent most of his time washing in the river rather than the waterfall so he could get off quickly to his job or his patrol duties. That meant the boy must do the journey at least once a day if not more.

As it was, today, in his excited Tim found he too climbed down rather fast, faster than he normally did anyway.

"So Tim, spot anything today?" Lauri asked.

"Not around here. Further north I did. At another pack."

"The pack you go to everyday?" Tim looked up. The man was shrewd there was no denying it. He had no idea the man had caught on about his old pack in the scarce conversations they had had. He never did elaborate and he certainly never shared the full story with anyone. Lauri definitely knew how to read between the lines. Something Tim took a mental note of.

"The very one or ones depending on how you look at it."

"I imagine you weren't too impressed to see someone lurking on territory you watch out for so closely."

"I killed the wolf. I warned him but he did not heed it. I left the body there so the packs know that they are being watched."

"Watched by an enemy or by you?"

That brought Tim up short. "By the enemy. I left it so they would know they were in danger and needed to increase their security."

"And in doing so you told them they had a protector. They must be wondering who it is."

"Hopefully they will put it down to a fight between two enemy wolves and double their guards."

"Or they now know someone is looking out for them and that they owe someone a debt of gratitude."

"No!" Tim whipped around to face Lauri. "I ask of nothing in return from anyone I help. I forbid anything in return from that particular pack."

"Got a few demons in your past then Tim?"

A hand clapped him on the shoulder and for some strange reason Tim took comfort in that hand. "I'm not proud of all my actions."

"The past shapes the present and the future. I don't think you have too much to be ashamed of."

"You do not know me."

"I know you better than you think. Collect your water the lad is back. And judging by his zig zagging he's brought enough to feed elephants not wolves."

Brendon did indeed come back with his arms piled high with meats and fruits that were wrapped in cloth and laying in bowls. He was out of breath carrying such a heavy load but he was smiling, pleased with himself for his errand.

"Thank you very much Brendon. I think this will feed us for at least a week."

"Nah, a day and a half tops. Just in case your mate isn't well enough to make it here tonight this should put you on until you can bring her tomorrow."

"Thank you." He said again. It seemed he was more than welcome to bring his mate along for dinner. Filling his pot up quickly he started to figure out how to not only carry all the food up the rocks but also his water. That was quickly solved when Lauri called forward to strong men who split the food between them and left some for Brendon to carry before all four started to climb the rocks again.

"I will see you as soon as my mate is well." Tim waved them goodbye and left the chatter and noise of the people below to themselves. He saw one of the females with her children around her. She had five and he still wondered how many more she would have after her sixth was born in maybe two months.

The men was diligent in their work of bringing food to the top. They didn't speak nor did they seem exerted in any way. Their faces were outlined with beards and their arms made up of roped muscle. They evidently still trained and the group dynamics were most likely still in play, even for rogues. He shook their hands and parted ways, hands filled goods.

He entered his house again with great difficulty having to put everything down before he was able to undo the door to his house. He wasted very little time in putting everything away and set the water to boil quickly over his stove, hurrying back up the stairs to see if she was alright. It was getting late afternoon by this point and he was debating waking her so she could eat something but it looked like this sleep was much needed. Still she could go back to sleep when she had eaten. Finally deciding that he would get her something he came back with a bowl of stew and gently taking hold of her arm he shook her a bit and waited for her reaction. She jumped a mile.

The first thing she knew as she was waking was that someone was not only touching her arm but they were shaking her. Lost for a moment in her own thoughts she almost screamed until she noticed that the hand wasn't hurting her. She was working herself up. She instantly remembered that she was with her mate and she turned to face him wondering why had had woken her. The bed she was in was rather comfortable and she wanted to stay in it a little longer but it wasn't hers so she hurriedly sat up and went to swing her legs out of it.

"No, it's ok, stay in bed. I'm just waking you so you can eat."

He sat on the edge of her bed and took in for a second time her appearance. Dishevelled as she was radiant her skin was clear and her eyes were bright though the ripped dress was a reminder all was not well. She was on alert from the moment of waking and she eyed up the bowl in his hands which he gave to her quickly. She was being quite restrained; he could tell she was eating as quickly as she could while not trying to look messy. He desperately wanted to know what had happened, he usually got a lot of information from the rogues he helped out.

"Are you willing to talk about what happened?"

"It's the same as what's been happening for a while. My pack got overrun, the alpha was challenged and he died, the one who challenged him took over our pack so we were little more than slaves. I ran when they killed the last of my family."

"I'm so sorry."

"Don't be, I know their death was inevitable, they've held control over us for four years now."

"Four years! Where are you from?"

"A weeks journey from here. I was told to make my way down to here as it's rumoured there is a merging of three packs that no one can get to. It's rumoured they're too protected too get into but I had to try. I had to run every day and night. I'm so tired and I couldn't stop for more than a half hour, they tried to follow me."

"You have brought them with you."

Her eyes widened, a sudden fear crossed her features and she dropped the spoon back in the bowl and stared at him afraid.

"I didn't mean to. I just wanted to get away," She hurried to explain.

"Hey, hey, it's alright. It's fine. Anyone would do the same. They are already here, they have been for eleven years but they haven't gotten very far."

"Are you angry at me?"

"No, not a bit. I can do a lot when I know what I am facing. It's when people keep things from me I get angry. It means more work for me when I eventually find out."

"What are you going to do to me?"

"I am going to offer you my bed and my home for as long as you need or want it. I will introduce you to my friends at the waterfall if you feel uncomfortable here. Either way you shall be protected. I will however say I don't want you travelling anymore while you are being followed and are now a particularly large target for them."

"That's it?"

"That's it. Oh and eat up, I'll get you seconds."

He patted her knee and left her to her thoughts. He was feeling a rage inside of him building. How dare someone kill her family?! How dare she be oppressed in her own pack by an outsider claiming to be alpha?! He clenched his fists as he filled up two more bowls and put sliced bread on a plate. He needed to calm down before he went back up to her but he was already calculating his chances and visualising the land trying to analyse it tactically and see what the odds were. What he needed to do. He knew the danger had just increased twicefold and it was up to him to sort it out. Not only was he a hidden target which he knew they were looking for but now his mate was a run away. He was sure their pack members were seeing prized gold if they went for Tim and his mate for the alpha.

He closed his eyes for a second. There was too much for him to do on his own. He knew that. Taking care of rogues and protecting three packs and a 'group' was hardly doing anything productive in the face of this atrocity. This situation would only be sorted with war. He needed to bring together an army worthy of this pack and the thought of war pained him dearly. For over eleven years this pack had been gathering, growing and taking over. He wondered how many were part of its ranks because they had no other option. Because their pack had been taken over and they were forced to serve under this new alpha. Innocents did not deserve to die in war.

He hit out at the nearest thing at him. A bowlful of stew. The bowl clattered to the floor, the wooden dish thumping dully as it hit the stone flooring. The contents seeped over the cracks and began running away from him.

"Mate?"

The soft, timid voice came from the top of his stairs. His woman, he cursed himself softly, the sound of the bowl falling to the floor would have startled her. "Tim?" She questioned hesitantly.

"Everything is fine. It's just me I knocked a dish off the table. I'll be up in a minute."

"May I come down?"

"Of course you can. If you are up to it, if you need rest though..." He trailed off. He didn't want to be one of those wolves who dictated what she do with every breath he had. He closed his eyes tight and stopped himself from being too possessive of her. If she took a turn for the worse he could easily carry her back to bed he reasoned with himself. Still he listened out carefully to make sure she got down the stairs on her own without falling or tripping. She did neither and came to the side of the house with his kitchen on. He didn't have a lot of walls, only the outside walls and structural supports. He liked open plans, it gave him optimal sight in case of an emergency and now it had more usefulness. She hadn't had to search to find him. He liked that.

"Oh." She said when she saw him fists clenched and eye closed with the bowl half way across the room and the stew on the floor. Her footsteps tapped lightly on the floor as she ran over grabbed a teacloth and was on her knees in seconds soaking up the liquid and picking up his bowl.

"You don't need to do that."

Tim bent down and tried to take the cloth from her hand but she patted his hand and smiled at him. "Sit down, you look stressed. I can clean the mess up."

"I made the mess, I should-;"

"Go."

He felt uncomfortable watching her clean his mess but she was very quick at it. "I had to serve the main table a lot. The leaders that ranked under the alpha were in charge, never the alpha. We saw him only when he challenged our pack's alpha. The leaders always made a mess." She found another bowl while Tim sat at the table watching her as if enchanted. Her graceful moves and nonchalant manner held him captive. Her hair whipped around as she moved. She needed another dress and he found himself picturing her body's frame underneath the white dress. Hair pins kept it in place and wrapped around her when the rips would have otherwise left her a little more on show.

She filled another dish up and paced it infront of him, he in turn pushed the already full bowl over to her and gave her first offerings of the bread plate.

"I don't need much more."

"You should, you've been running a week."

"Thank you for dinner."

Silence took over, she didn't like to stare at him but found she couldn't help but take sneaky glances in his direction. It was still a shock to see that she had a mate and she was desperately wondering just how much her life as going to change now. As it was she didn't think she wanted to leave him, let alone his house. He had a dark and brooding edge to him that had her wondering what his story was. His facial hair told her he was a man of power himself and she felt the ripple of wolven strength and command about him that she couldn't help but want to huddle up against. She wanted that strength and she admired that strength in him, she wanted him to command her, she felt herself slowly starting to desire submitting to him and letting him protect her.

That in itself was scary. She had run from dominating males and now she was sensing another and craving it. As she took another bite of stew, tasting his cooking, he also felt different. That evil and warmongering that had a stench pouring from the wolves back at her home was a distant memory when confronted with her mate. He smelt fresh. Like water. Like fresh water clinging to the air in the early morning. And she felt him all around the house. She smelt his scent everywhere. It was like the very house was actually him the walls oozed his scent.

Then she took a look around. The house was shaped and smoothed entirely from wood. She took note of the bowl she had picked up and discarded for a clean one, the make shift stove that was little more than a mound of stone with a fire on top, over which he hooked on a large pot. It had the old world feel to it that came with lack of resources. He was literally living out here, in the wild. He had made the little luxuries he had.

"You built this place didn't you?"

Her incredulous tone had him snapping his head up to her eyes to assess whether she thought that a good thing or a bad thing. But what he did see in her eyes surprised more than finding a mate did. He had felt inadequate bringing her back to this rough life but her eyes were lit up with pride.

"Yes I made it." He answered slowly.

"Oh my, this is so good. You are so skilled in this. Have you ever thought of doing this as a job."

"I work part time as a mechanic. So not really."

"You should, you could maybe set up your own business doing this. This is wonderful. It's like living a dream. Having the simple things in life, I bet you have a lot of satisfaction using what you make."

"I was very proud when I first made it, now it's just the norm for me."

"How long did it take you to build?"

"About three months, working every day and most of the night."

"Wow, it must have kept you entertained."

"It did. I had just finished school and could only start my apprenticeship in the garage in the September so I had a few free months. It kept me occupied when I would have gone mad instead."

"Finished school. You were sixteen when you made this?"

Again the tone of her voice had him assessing her first before answering. Her eyes were wide as she heard him speaking. "I am strong for my age." He commented.

"But where is your family?" Shame ran through his veins like cold water forcing him to turn away from her. "I ran from them."

"Why? Did they abuse you? Were they horrible?" He cringed. He actually felt like she had slapped him. Standing from the table he picked up the dirty and used dishes and took it to a basin of water to clean them. Ignoring his father he thought of the family he had left behind. "No, they were everything one could ask of a family."

"Then why did you leave?"

Good question he thought. Eleven years on, he still wondered; why did he actually leave them?

CHAPTER 4

"I never did ask you your name. Forgive me, I ask now." Hastily changing the subject he turned back to her, she was puzzled at the abrupt change but said nothing. "Eveliina."

"What a beautiful name. Eveliina." It practically rolled off his tongue.

"Thanks."

"Well, I think it's time you got back in bed, you need to sleep. First though, where are you hurt?"

"I'm not hurt."

"I smell blood."

"It's only my arm." She blushed a little. She had fallen on day three and as she had fallen she had scraped it along the floor, unfortunately the floor had been covered with lots of tony stones that grazed her skin. It stung but there was only dotted blood and no deep cuts. She was embarrassed that he was probably thinking she was real damsel, wounded and needing to be repaired by her man.

Shoving up her shirt roughly she showed him her grazes expecting him to nod and forget about such a trivial thing. It shocked her though because he took her arm gently in his hand and assessed it for a minute before finding a cloth and dipping it into a bowl of boiled and cooled water. Very carefully he wiped it over her arm removing the traces of dried blood and dirt that she had tried to cover by pulling her sleeve down. He tried not to hurt her further but the dried blood didn't just wipe off. He took his time rubbing at the blood softly so it wouldn't tug at her tender skin, finding that he didn't like to see her in even the tiniest amount of pain. Pulling out some of his homemade cream that he often used on own wounds he smoothed the paste –like substance over the cuts. Finally he took some gauze from his little emergency medical kit and bandaged her arm up. It would be fine in the morning but he wanted her to heal a little more with no pain. It was with barely any pressure he placed his hand over her bandaged arm to signal he was done and then he pulled back down her sleeve to hide her injury again.

"Sleep well Eveliina."

Eveliina went to sleep that late afternoon with his tiny bowed head in her mind. She had thought he would be expecting a terrible gash or something yet what made it so special was that it was nothing of the sort but he still gave to her the attention and patience that should only have been due a serious injury. She felt cherished and protected, it was like she actually mattered in the world and after living as a servant for years it was a feeling that had long ago been taken away from her. She never though she would feel wanted or needed again and here was Tim rekindling in her a hope and determination for life.

"I think you should see this."

"Lead the way."

Ray followed the warrior infront of him through the forest towards one of the more dense locations around. He smelt it before he saw it. Blood. Two wolves' blood. On the floor spread out and dead however was a single wolf - a werewolf whom Ray did not recognise. He sighed walking closer up to it and crouching down to see it properly.

"Not one of ours." He told the little gathering of wolves from nearby. Ray was taking in every mark on the wolf and the skin under its claws. It had fiercely been trying to kill someone. "No one reported seeing anything or being attacked?" Ray confirmed. The shaking of heads and murmurs of 'no' only made him sigh. It was the same way of killing as what he had seen by the lake elven years ago. The wolves were still coming for his pack. He had to inform the other Alpha's. And Tendra, he never left Tendra out of anything, especially as Christopher was turning eighteen soon. The lad wanted to be a warrior and he was good enough to be one. While Ray felt like every father; the terrible anxiety, he was proud that his only son was following in his footsteps. Tendra had also had the mixed feelings so they made a deal. She supported her son through whatever he wanted but she was to be informed every single step of the way at just what he was getting into. The new killing counted as a threat which meant Tendra should know about it. As did the mysterious killer who had protected them, on two occasions now. Two out of many Ray was thinking.

He stood up from his crouch, there was nothing more to be done. "Burn it." He ordered before turning and walking back. He went a little further to the left to follow the pattern of the trees that would eventually get him on the path, it was a little longer home but it gave him more time to spend thinking about how to word such news to Tendra. She was a strong woman, used to bad news but he still liked to tell her gently. His foot crunched on a fallen leaf and he looked down, it was summer the leaves did not fall off unless something disturbed them. He cast a curious glance down, not really too bothered by the leaf but what he saw and what he smelled was something else entirely different.

Crouching back down to the floor he saw droplets of blood, five of them, dried now under the sun and due to the time gone by since they fell. The scent was subtle, hard to catch because of the length of time wasted but still it caught his attention.

"Looks like our saviour bled for us."

Tim slept fitfully that night, the heat of the night made it so that he didn't want to be either clothed or have a thick heavy quilt on him. He usually slept naked but with a female guest he had pulled on pants just in case she came into his room for any strange reason, such as fear or curiosity. But he was too warm and if he threw off his quilt he wasn't 'cosy' or comfy. Instead he tried to angle the quilt half on and half off his body but as he turned with his restlessness the quilt slid off his body and he had to readjust it.

In short he tossed and turned and grumbled the night away until by the time the birds woke him up in the morning he was unrested and in a mood. He groaned on waking up knowing he had to get to work and he hadn't taken his mate to the waterfall, nor had he given her the food they had cooked. He had strangely felt the need to prepared food himself, for her to taste his cooking. It seemed that the mating instinct had intervened yesterday but today it would not.

He woke up and went to his kitchen where he laid out the food from yesterday which was still wrapped up and in various dishes. Writing a letter on a scrap piece of paper even he was surprised to see laying around he told Eveliina to eat as much as she liked and to explore his house as she wanted. He had to go to work but would be back by early afternoon. Snagging up food for himself he both ate some and took some with him before going on his run through the forest to his waterfall. This morning he was greeted by many people.

He wasn't use to the blatant turnout, usually they let him shower and get on his way. Men came over to him as he scrubbed his body, his fingers trailing over his worst scare. They chatting away to him, laughed even and engaged him in the pleasantries he found himself secretly craving. Usually they left him to be by himself, he got on with his routine of washing and hurrying on to his various duties. Today was different however and he wasn't going to complain. While his isolation no longer got him down as it had in the beginning he was still a man and wolf; he craved conversation as a man but as a wolf it worse, he craved a pack, a family.

"Did you try the food?" One of the men shouted to him.

"Oh yes, it was delicious. Whoever made the pie, really that was best thing I've eaten in months. I'll be having more of that when I go back."

"Are you going to bring your mate tonight?"

"Yeah, it will be about seven."

"That's fine." Lauri nodded appearing suddenly and smiling. Brendon was no where to be seen that morning and Tim wouldn't go without seeing to the boy safety.

"I haven't yet seen Brendon." He told Lauri who beamed all the more at the question.

A little tap on his back by something scratchy but not too harsh had Tim turning and swatting at what was aggravating his skin. Expecting a piece of foliage or something he jumped a little as he came face to face with a young man hanging upside down on the rocks sand tickling him with his own shower scrub.

"Brendon, now I see you."

"I snuck up on you, your skills are waning."

"My skills are just fine I'll have you know, this waterfall is the problem."

"You can't blame the waterfall for your lack of hearing."

"No? How about your wet clothes?" Taking the lad completely off guard Tim picked him up off the rocks and dunked him unceremoniously in the water. Laughing he let go of the lad and watched him come to the surface spluttering and glaring.

"No fair, you caught me off guard."

"Now whose skills are lacking?" Tim gave out a belly laugh and launch after the lad who squealed and tried to run off, resulting in a kind of jump start swimming/sinking motion that only made the teen swallow water. Feeling water slid into his mouth and down his throat Brendon panicked a little, flailing his arms around in a desperate attempt to push the water away and propel himself more fully above the surface. Hands wrapped around his waist, firm hands that turned him so his face was facing the sky and then began to carry him out of the water while at the same time patting his back. Tim wore a wry grin on his face as he carried the choking Brendon and himself out of the water and set them both on the rocks to dry.

Tim was still laughing and Brendon blushed to see they had themselves a nice little audience of smirking residents. Lifting a hand Tim went to ruffle the lad's hair only to be hit from behind and thrown face first to the floor. He grunted as his face scraped on the rocks around him. The weight on his back did not let up and he turned, curious to see what Brendon was doing, only to find the kid had stretch himself out over Tim and was sunning himself under the direct glare of the sun – using Tim as a deckchair.

"Cheeky little thing, off my back." Tim said wiggling a little. "For such a skinny thing, you're starting to weight a bit."

Brendon turned around and stuck out his tongue at Tim before getting up and holding out a hand to Tim. They laughed along with each other before Tim knew he had no choice but to get to work.

"I'm sorry I have to go. I'll get you back tonight though." With a friendly wave at everyone else he made his way back up the rocks and ran off to work. He would do a loop of his old pack before going back for Eveliina that night.

A trail of men followed him up the rocks and nodded goodbye to him as he parted way. The run to work had him sweating out but he looked no different than usual, his boss was used to him turning up in low ridden jeans and only a vest top on when he greeted customers. That same vest top was taken off when he was working on the cars. The boss now only shook his head at Tim's lack of clothing, something Tim often smirked at.

Three cars were already booked in a waiting by the time he strolled in. "Morning." He called to his boss. "Morning." Grabbing his tool belt he reached the first car lifted the bonnet and began. Within the hour he had grease all over his hands and he was constantly wiping at the sweat on head thanks to the summer heat so his face was getting grubbier as the morning progressed. He grabbed a stained cloth and wiped the oil and grease of his hands as best as he could so he could sign some paperwork and then was under one of the cars with a spanner in one hand and his feet sticking out at the bottom. Whistling away to a random tune in his head his mind drifted so his was completely calm and content not even thinking about his wolf life while he acted in this human life. He enjoyed the sixteen hours a week he did. He was allowed to be a different person. One without so many cares in the world.

Pottering away he finished up and got from under the car, wiping his hands again and was just about to write his signature on the paperwork when he noticed a scent he hadn't smelt before, and a silence that bothered him. Tim was a whistler, always had been but his boss Tony was a heavy footed man who was always here there and everywhere. Tony was up and down most days always finding something to do and looking incredibly busy even when there was no work to be done. So why where his footsteps being missed today?

"Tony?" Keeping hold of his spanner he went on alert immediately, ears pricked up Tim felt the wolf strength in him travelling along his bloodstream and through his muscles making him aware of his instinct and build. Side stepping around the car he made his way to the office and it was times like this that he was glad the garage was open plan, save for the office, and all was on the ground floor. He reached the door and immediately noticed that paper was flying and the blinds had been drawn. Tony never drew the blinds, he liked to make sure his workers were working and not slacking off for long periods of time.

Tim looked to the door handle to see that it wasn't fully locked. This was deliberate. Everything looked staged. He already knew what he would see when he walked in and though he knew that it didn't prepare him. Pushing open the door Tony was sat on the floor with back against the wall, legs outstretched infront of him and hands limp on the floor. Across his neck and over the wall was blood.

CHAPTER 5

His instincts took over, the wolf in him coming out sharp. His eyes glared open checking his surroundings, under the car and behind the huge mechanics that could very easily conceal a person. At first he didn't notice that his appearance had changed until he noticed he was walking with a bounce to his steps and his head was cocked to the side. For the first time he was partially changing, his wolf coming out at the sense of threat and attack, and so caught up in the moment Tim hadn't realised that he was slowly losing control.

Loss of control would help nothing and he had calmed his breathing down to let the anger he was feeling fade away. Choosing a form with which to walk around with his human side came back to him. A customer could easily come in with their car and Tim wouldn't be able to explain the presence of a wolf. The garage which was completely ground floor turned out to be empty save for Tim and his dead boss. The attack had been done on purpose, Tony's neck slashed with the claws of a wolf made it impossible for Tim to go to the police about this. He felt a pang of guilt to the wife and children that Tony had waiting back at home for him.

They could never find his body and he just hoped that they found closure in some other way.

Closing the shop he picked up Tony's body and walked to the outskirts of a forest, any forest, it wasn't the one Tim lived in but it would do; there was no pack on most of this land for quite a while. Tim had a lot of freedom. He buried his friend in the ground, deep down, spending hours digging deep with his claws in his wolf form. After that he scooped the earth back up and placed it over the body. The sense of warning was clear, Tim had been reprimanded by this wayward pack and they were warning him not to get mixed up in their business but to submit to them. Something he wasn't going to do.

He spent the next hour clearing the blood from the office and tidying it up. He wanted a UV light to ensure that no blood traces could be found but he hadn't gotten one so he sighed and went back over the room for a fourth time. He was meticulous - humans could not get involved in his world. They couldn't be trusted to know the workings of a wolf pack and not want to either kill them or experiment on them. Ray had had human connections but they were rare, Tim himself didn't want to get mixed up in that kind of thing.

The thought of Ray brought back to his mind his old pack, the three that joined it and he felt like cold water had just been dumped on him. Ashton. The name hurt to say, even to whisper. As Ray had taken over the role of a father so too had Ashton. He even called him Uncle Ashton. The man had lost so much as well but Tim had always been there for him as he had for Tim. Leaving had not been easy decision, staying away was even harder. But now he knew he couldn't go back. He knew he wouldn't be welcome anymore. Still, the thought that all those he loved as family, even they didn't think that of him, was more painful than he could imagine.

He left his boss once he was buried and let his wolf run a while. The feel of his muscles stretching was pleasant. It was a welcome relief to his body and the heavy feel of his long shaggy hair around him made him feel protected. He had always clutched a wolf teddy as a child and when he first changed he was pretty impressed that he was now the 'teddy' he took comfort in. The same comfort was still there now, though not as childishly had it had once been. He knew that his body could fight and run. He was safe while he was like this. His large paws hit the ground as he covered miles in but a few bounds. The forest was dense and the years of exploring and familiarity could easily been seen because he knew what to doge and when it was coming up. He made his way through the trees and bushes, brambles and weeds and thorns as if he was walking along a street avoiding lampposts. It was natural to him. The sounds of insects were loud in his ears, the chirping and the clicking tried to distract him but he was going somewhere important. He was going to his old pack.

The smell of them relaxed his wolf. There was no fresh scent of blood. There was no wounded and pained cries. All sounded and smelt fine. He let himself just take that in for a moment and breathe a sigh of relief. They were alright.

He edged closer to the start of their territory. Knowing full well he was trespassing and needed to be as quiet as possible he crouched low to the ground. Today he was pleased to sense the scent of Ray. And more than that was the scent of Lebon, Myco and Aliysha. That meant that the allied alphas had come together to survey the situation, the wolf had been found and the strong scent of alpha blood would be a slight deterrent. That did also mean that checking on them was going to take him a little longer as he dodged their patrols but... challenge accepted.

Smiling he made his way into the forest. He hoped he did not see his brother in law Ray, but at the same time he would never let his shame get in the way of protecting them. His youth had been spent wandering around those four packs and he wouldn't abandon them now. Extra guards had been placed around the area; Tim observed from a distance that there was both an inner ring and an outer ring of warriors standing guard. He stayed long enough to notice that every fifteen minutes a midway guard would march through the territory creating a constant moving third ring of surveillance. On the whole this was a brilliant guard. Tim was very pleased with it. For a while he sat in one of the trees observing the guard and figuring out a way into the camp unnoticed. He was very, very, pleased to see that it took him a long time to figure that out.

He edged around the outer ring and took to sniffing the air for intruders, when he wasn't as worried for Eveliina's safety he would investigate further but tonight he wanted to get home to make sure she was safe. His old pack was for now. He scented nothing. He allowed himself to see the familiar steel safe house and the children that played on the sand and gravel around before turning away. The safe house, which most lived in, had an underground passage in case of emergencies. It was complete with electricity and the whole area held such a large and secure community he knew that they would be alright if attacked. Turning he ran back to his own home determined that the minute the sun came up the following morning he would be back at this forest doing a full a scout.

His house was quiet - it was a strange thing because after this afternoon he felt like silence was a bad thing. He was on edge, his muscles coiled and ready, his wolf inches from surfacing. For all he knew though nothing was wrong. The smell of food was reassuring and once inside he saw the food on the table. He could see that Eveliina had eaten some though which was good but she wasn't downstairs and he panicked.

Running through his little house he searched the ground floor and then upstairs, she was gone. Completely gone, his heart was thumping him from the inside out, beating at him until he thought it would kill him. The fire in the kitchen had burned out – a good thing on such a warm day but it meant that no one had tended it in a while.

He was starting to feel lost, starting to hyperventilate as he contemplated gruesome ways to kill the animals that dared to take his mate, when singing made him whip his head around and he came face to face with Eveliina carrying a basket of flowers and walking through his front door.

"Oh you're back, I went out to gather some flowers. You don't have a lot of personal items in the house so I thought flowers would brighten it up a little."

"I worried about you."

"I did not go far." He looked at the blue and purple flowers in her hands, scattered through the dark colours were bright orange bulbs not blossomed yet.

"You went too far anyway."

"I'm sorry."

She said it before she thought properly and then she was angry at herself for apologising; she was her own person, allowed to do what she wanted and when she wanted.

"In fact, no I'm not. I thought flowers would be a nice thing to bring you for your home and you're shouting at me all ready. I've known you a day and already you try to dictate to me where is too far to go!"

"I was whistling away underneath a car today when my boss was murdered by the wolves that follow you. I am also a target to them and I come home worried sick thinking they have found you as they did my boss and you are not here. I worry Eveliina and tell you not to go too far because I know who is hunting us!"

His raised his voice. He actually shouted. It was the only time in his life he had ever shouted at someone and it didn't feel all that good. The wolves he killed had been given but a whispered warning before they disobeyed him. He did not shout, he lived life trying to make peace not frighten people or upset them. And here he was, upsetting his own mate. He felt bad the minute his rant was over.

"I'm sorr-;"

"Don't, I'm sorry, I guess I had no idea what sort of day you have had."

"You weren't to know."

Wandering over to the kitchen he picked up another piece of pie and offered it first to Eveliina who declined it and then ate it for himself.

"I'm sorry," she said, "It's just that... mates come with rules."

"Mates come with protection." He reasoned back and then shook his head. "But I know I can't take from you your freedom. I'm sorry for overreacting but I am very afraid for you right now."

"We need to get to know each other." Eveliina declared. Mating was inevitable. It was like the sea: better to swim alongside the current rather than fighting it.

"We will. There is time yet. For now, there are people I want you to meet. I told them I would be there for seven but I don't think they will mind us being early. Not when I explain what has happened. I want you protected. There are only two women here but there are three young children who are females. Everyone else is male, I'm sorry but rogues are rarely female."

"There were rogue children?!"

"A few but some are products of mates finding the women at the waterfall."

Eveliina looked down at her dress, it left much to be desired. "I don't look good for meeting new people."

"I have not the time to take you shopping, I am very sorry." Walking over he picked up her hand. "I will get you a dress as soon as I can, I am sure that Rebekah will see you clothed for the time being."

"It's ok; I don't expect you to buy me things. I will get a job-;"

"You will do no such thing; I have plenty of money, as you can see given my rustic living I don't spend much of my wage. I make what I need and buy only a few other items."

That was an argument for another day Eveliina decided. "Come on." He motioned for her to follow him and led her out of the cabin. The journey to the waterfall took him twenty minutes at a run every morning but it took almost an hour at walking pace. He didn't want to push his mate since she was still recovering from exhaustion and he was constantly alert, always listening for even the slightest thing that might be 'off'. Eveliina couldn't help but watch him, his footsteps were calculated, each and every placement was due to careful consideration of footprints and body angle, and each step he took ensured that he was angled to cover her in case of attack. Even his feet were placed at the optimum place in case he suddenly needed to defend them both.

At last the sound of crashing water took over from the tense silence that had emerged between the two of them and Eveliina felt herself relax. Tim had told her of the waterfall but when they emerged from the trees she was still shocked by it. It was a the size of a six storey building, the water was faster than she thought possible and it seemed to fall into thin air bearing down on large boulder sized rocks and wearing them down miniscule bit at a time. In years the rocks would erode away she knew that but it would take many, many years. Still the power of water was incredible to see, she didn't fancy standing in the river that led to the waterfall; she would be swept off within seconds.

Unaware that her fingers had squeezed Tim's hand as she held it, she felt him tighten his fingers around her and start to lead her towards the usual rock he started off with.

"We're climbing down?!" He almost laughed at how high her voice had managed to get.

"There are no built-in stairs."

"I think you should put you wood making skills to good use then and create a stairwell."

"That would end up being rather convenient for our enemies."

She stared wide eyed at the way down. It was a long way to fall and it wouldn't be an easy fall either, the rocks jutted out at all angles so she would be pummelled by them before even reaching the bottom.

"Eveliina, do you trust your mate?"

"I don't know you well enough to trust you yet."

"You followed me through a dangerous forest."

"I didn't see the danger."

"Regardless. You followed me through there, now follow me down here. I promise to protect you with my life."

She stared at the 'hole in the earth' for a long time before clutching onto his bicep and swallowing. "If I fall, I'm taking you with me. So don't let me fall."

"I don't intend to. Now, would you rather climb down yourself or do you want to go over my shoulder?" He couldn't help but smirk at the end of that, it was either smirk or burst out laughing.

"I might be scared but I still have some pride!" She lightly smacked him on his arm playfully and strutted forward.

"Oh no you don't!" He caught her arm and pulled her behind him. "I go first."

Placing a foot on the rock first he bent his knees as if to sit down but he used his lowered position to reach sideways to another rock taking hold of it and easing himself down to the next 'shelf'. Turning back he lifted up his arm to guide Eveliina's hands to the finger holds and ease her down alongside him. Her body slid against his as he stood close to her, ensuring she was as close to the rocks as could be. He shivered at the feel of her skin to close to his and the curve of her bottom sliding along him to fit expertly in his embrace.

"See that wasn't so bad." He said once she stopped fidgeting.

Keeping her always infront of him and facing the wall of rocks he went first and guided her body down step by step always keeping hold of some body part and not letting her stand for more than a few seconds while he made his own way down for fear that she would fall. On a few occasions she went to look down at the height they had left to climb but he stopped her, putting his arm at the side of her head and caging her head in with his biceps so she saw only the rock she held onto. He knew she would panic if she saw the long way down and a flailing woman so high up was not going to help in keeping her from harm.

When at last he touched the bottom rock, the small one that told him he was on the ground floor he breathed a sigh of relief —one of many so far that day. He had never felt so scared for anyone. He knew he wouldn't let her fall and yet his mind had screamed at him to be even more careful than he already was being.

He didn't let her climb down the last rock he simply reached up and wrapped his hands around her waist picking her up and lowering her screaming form to the floor. "You could have warned me!"

"I like that you put your arms around my neck when you spooked." He turned away from her to greet the sudden crowd that had gathered behind them.

"Well the screaming woman is my mate Eveliina."

CHAPTER 6

Well she would get him back for that cheek. She was thinking of all the things she could do to pay him back for scaring her and using it to his advantage when one strong muscled arm wound back around her waist. "Eveliina meet the waterfall rogues."

"Very pleased to meet you Eveliina, my name is Lauri."

The man infront of Tim bowed ever so slightly to her and the glisten in his eye was something she had seen before. No wolf bowed to another unless of high statue. She narrow her eyes at him, about to question his motive for that little gesture but as Tim was looking the other way, greeting someone else, Lauri put a finger to his mouth. She took the hint and stayed silent.

"Tim, you're early. You know food won't be ready."

"I'm not only here for food." Clipping Brendon lightly across the head Tim shook his head in mock exasperation. The kid laughed.

"What you here so early for then?"

"You wanted to see my mate. Here she is."

The young man was suddenly bouncing. "Another female, cool, Suzie and Rebekah will be happy, now they won't torment me so much. Hi, I'm Brendon."

"Eveliina,"

"Please to meet you. Come on, follow me, I'll show you some of the others." Tim had no say in the matter and Eveliina allowed herself to be carried off despite the fact that Brendon never asked Tim for permission and simply took his mate away. Stunned at the fact he been made mateless in such an easy manner he turned to Lauri who was laughing quietly.

"Best keep an eye on that one,"

"I intended to."

Sniggers burst out around Tim and he noticed then that he had an audience. "Hello." He nodded to them all. A chorus of 'hello' greeted him. "Lauri," He lowered his voice, letting the man know he wanted privacy.

"Come to my rock," The man said.

"My boss was killed today, while I was in the building." Tim started as soon as they were sat in privacy.

"What?"

"I was under a car and I smelt something funny. Getting up I noticed it was too quiet for my boss. I went to the office and found him dead."

"What did you do with him?"

"Took him deep into the forest and buried him, cleaned the office and phoned the police to say he went missing after he left for lunch."

"Good damage control. Bad situation."

"I didn't hear a thing, that's bad Lauri. I should have been more alert. I use my human job as a means of acting human. Of finding space and solace, I know now I can't do that. I need to be on guard at all times. I failed."

"You can't think like that. You need a reprieve from all the good you do Tim. You need a break at some point; you will only wear yourself down if you don't. You can't see this as a failure - just learn from it."

"My boss died because I wasn't prepared. I foolishly thought they would not harm my human connections. I did not think they would use them against me and I was arrogant enough to think that I would be able to protect them if it did come down to that. I lay on my back fixing a car and whistled while my boss was being murdered!"

Lauri looked at Tim for a second, he was red in the face, it was evident he had kept this emotion in for a while as he saw to the needs of his mate and he needed to get out his own self anger.

"Then learn from this mistake and prepare for attacks coming in all directions, even the ones you thought unlikely."

"That's why I'm early; I wanted Eveliina in the protection of this society."

"Society?"

"Yes, this... This. I don't know what you call yourselves."

Lauri got that glisten in his eyes again. Time to tell Tim the obvious that had eluded him for years now.

"We call ourselves a pack Tim."

"But you're rogues."

"We were rogues. We stay here because we formed a pack."

"Then who is Alpha?"

"Guess.."

The tone of Lauri voice had Tim stiffening, he could not be meaning what Tim thought he was.

"You?" He asked hesitantly.

"No, I've become a leader to everyone here in the absence of the Alpha. I take the role of Beta."

"Absolutely not."

"I can't be beta?"

"No, I can not be Alpha!"

He jumped to his feet. He had never agreed to this. He saw rogues to safety, he picked their brains for information. He was a protector. That was his role. He protected the land around his old pack and now his own home and anyone else who needed it. He was a guardian of wolves, not an Alpha. He was a lone wolf, a rogue himself with a past he was sorely ashamed of.

"I can not be alpha." He declared.

"What are the duties of an Alpha, Tim?" Lauri asked him, his wise face hardened in seriousness and disapproval at Tim blatant denial.

"To protect their pack and to provide for their pack. To ensure the pack thrives and to fight for their pack - to the death if necessary."

"And what have you done for us Tim?"

"Ignored you!" He cried out. He had not been a good alpha to them. He had lived in his own bubble as he had for eleven years. He had been self-sufficient and damn it he had whistled his way through part time work as a mechanic and exercised out his demons by weight training to ignore the past that caused him sleepless nights.

"You clothed us. You fed us. You introduced each and every one of us to each other and provided us with the safest place for shelter you knew of. You run patrols every day and check on us at least once a day. When we have no food you give us some. You share your money with us. In short Tim you have been to us, an alpha, and under the aid of you we learnt to become a pack. We did not want to be a pack. We wanted to run forever and leave behind the atrocities that held us previously. You Tim, you, pulled us together and formed us into a pack. Unknowingly, yes. But you created the bond. It been almost complete for years. The other day you found your mate and it was finally strong and very, very much complete."

"I...I only meant to help you. I never meant to be your alpha."

"We all know that. But everything happens for a reason and we found that we felt safer near to you; we got along with everyone who came here and most stayed to become a pack member... under you. We kept it from you for years because you weren't ready to hear this truth. You needed the solitude you pushed onto yourself."

"Then what has changed? What has made you suddenly decide to tell me that I have yet more responsibility in this world?"

"Simple; you brought your mate to us for her protection. Your wolf instincts made it so you willingly gave her up to the pack you knew would die to save her."

His legs gave out. Weak from his new found knowledge Tim sat down. "I am unworthy of being an alpha."

"I have known you ten years Tim, you have proved that worth every day I've known you."

"I have done things I'm not proud of."

"So have we all. We all have pasts that shape us into who we are today Tim, and it's the present and future we concentrate on. Let your past be your lesson and learn from it, so in the future you can be the best person possible."

"I am a coward."

"You fight the east wayward pack. That is not cowardly."

"I abandoned my family!"

"Then don't let it be in vain. You have a new one here, don't abandon this one."

Lauri stood up and left Tim to his contemplations. There was only so much one could say to a confused wolf before silence and isolation had to commence for the wolf to work things out.

He wasn't proud of keeping such a big thing from Tim but if this was the reaction when he was ready, he hated to think what his reaction would have been when he was younger and even less ready. At twenty six though Tim now needed to be even more adult.

CHAPTER 7

He had made up his mind. Two hours of sitting in the waning light contemplating everything he had done and everything he had wanted to accomplish in life had told Tim everything he needed to know. That he was an alpha and if he thought he wasn't good enough – then tough; he had no choice but to become good enough. These people needed him and if they had thought him alpha for years and he hadn't been there for them then he had some making up to do. He wouldn't let them down again.

He wouldn't let leaving his family be for nothing either. He would take this alpha business as a destiny he couldn't achieve in Ray's pack. It was the only comfort he was ever going to get, to think like that, and he held onto it with greedy hands. He at least needed to make sure he tried. Stepping out of the rock felt different. He felt taller as he stepped out into the open and he automatically raised his head a little more and straightened his back. He didn't notice for a minute that his pack were watching him entering their fold. It was only as he passed the first man that he noticed that the man had dropped to one knee that and his eyes widened.

"You are being honoured as an Alpha Tim. This is a courtesy that occurs when an alpha comes into his own. Welcome to the pack. We greet you gladly."

The old formal words at the end made him feel like warm liquid was flowing through his veins. It was the feeling of acceptance that warmed Tim and he looked at the kneeling man with an affection he had never thought possible. It was like looking at a little brother even though the man kneeling had to be at least, if not older, than Tim's age. He felt protective of this kneeling man, as if he had to care for him and watch over him... he knew now what it felt like to be an alpha. If felt like looking at lots of baby Christopher's on their first night home and whispering into their ears that he would always be there for them.

The feeling was overwhelming. One by one the pack infront of him knelt and accepted his authority and protection. They took their places as official pack members and Tim held onto the arms of Lauri as both a guide and anchor and older brother. This was a different bond; the one between alpha and beta. Lauri felt older, wiser, a consultant in matters. It felt like Tim had a good solid friend in Lauri and knew he would confide in this man absolutely. But he also felt protective, fiercely so but not in a newborn baby way - in a growling best friend way.

"liking the forming bonds?" Lauri smirked.

"It feels... good. Like family."

"We are your family."

"You feel like it."

He took one last look at his pack before looking at Lauri again.

"You are wanting to see your only equal. The one who feels the bonds the same way as you do."

"Am I?" Was that what he was missing?

"She is over here."

Lauri led Tim over to the little group of young ones and the two females that stood by them. Eveliina wasn't there and Tim looked at Lauri puzzled. A little cough signalled at the women to part and standing there in a dark, lapis lazuli shade of blue and one armed, dress was Eveliina. She had her hands clasped tightly together and was waiting for something. It looked like approval.

"Are you going to accept your mate as female alpha?" Lauri asked.

"Of course!"

"Then go to her, you're keeping her waiting."

Unaware of protocol he strode forward until he reached her and trusted his instincts to do what needed. He picked up her hands so they weren't clasped together and then he leant down and kissed her gently on the lips. "Why did I never see Ray do this?" He questioned.

"He was already Alpha, his initiation had been done before you saw him, no doubt." Lauri replied. "And the accepting of a female alpha is not always done with a crowd. We were just being nosey."

Taking a playful swipe at Lauri he noticed the formalities must be over as everyone was laughing and moving around freely again. "Thank a lot." He said sarcastically.

"No probs, Alpha."

"I prefer Tim."

"Get use to Alpha."

Everyone walked off, leaving Tim and Eveliina alone together.

"You look beautiful."

"Thanks, it was Rebekah's but she had never worn it so she let me have it."

"I will buy you some clothes of your own tomorrow."

"It's alright don't worry." She took hold of his hand and turned them both so they were facing the waterfall. "This place is beautiful."

"Yes, it is. Though I don't live here myself."

"Why not?"

"I built my cabin before I saw this place, and my cabin is placed in a crossroads of sorts, more rogues would pass by the cabin than the waterfall and my aim was to aid the rogues and get information from them, as much as they could give me anyway."

"So you won't live here yourself?"

"I don't know Eveliina, I never meant to become the alpha here. I meant to give a sort of sanctuary to those who needed it, creating a pack was never on my mind."

"You can do a lot of good as the alpha of a pack though."

"Yes, I intend to do that now."

A cold breeze blew her hair to the side and she shivered under the unexpected coldness. Tim wound an arm around her shoulders and his body heat warmed her up a little so she snuggled into his body.

"So for eleven years you have been alone?"

"Yes."

"Why?" He hadn't really discussed this with anyone. Lewis had been his best friend growing up and the loss of his best friend had been hard at first to cope with. With no one to talk to and plan things with he had felt a little lost until the solitude had become an independence to him.

"I can go where I like and do what I want with no questions asked. I lead kind of a double life, in the forest I protect, in the human world I fix things. I enjoyed the freedom both lives gave me. I knew that if rogues came past me they would not want to stay where I do. I am not in the safest location but it's hidden, partially anyway. Being part of a pack didn't seem to be compatible with the life I wanted to lead."

"Do you regret creating this pack?"

"No, I never knew I had created it until today. I try not to regret anything in life though there are things I am not proud of."

He fell silent, he wasn't ready to tell what he had done in his past just yet. He just wanted to hold her knowing it might be all he was able to do for a while. He had never even dated a woman, he had been too focused as a young teen in training and excelling physically and mentally and by the time hormones had fully set in he was alone in the world with little chance of meeting any females. So this whole experience was foreign to him. He didn't know quite what to do, how to behave, how to woo her and gain her trust. He had been given to Ashton most of his life when his sister Tendra and Alpha Ray had been getting together flirting, dating amongst other things.

In the end he figured that he would go by instinct, as he did most things. He would do what came naturally to him. It had seemed to work so far. "I smell food," He said, "Go and find the women and I'm sure they'll make you feel welcome." Sensing that he wanted some alone time Eveliina left him standing by the water.

Bending down he untied his shoes and slipped them off his feet, next he took off his socks and rolled up his trousers to his knees. Stepping lightly into the water he let it lap over his feet as the waterfall pushed it past him. The water had a little heat to it thanks to the sun but it was still cool on his feet. He was about to stand there contemplating things, mulling the day he had, had over in his mind but he was not given that freedom.

As a man who was constantly on guard he was very soon pulled from his reverie as in the distance he smelt familiar smell. The hair on his back stood on its end. His shoulder muscles flexed.

Fire. No more a pondering alpha he instead was crouched in the water. He was no longer letting the water flow past instead he was feeling it; the way it moved, that rhythm it had. He locked onto the temperature of it so he understood how his body would react submerged in it. He deemed it the perfect temperature. Cool enough to keep him alert, warm enough to keep his muscle from freezing or spasming. The current was fast, it always was with that sharp fall it endured but his muscles were strong enough to swim alongside it.

Today he would scout with added purpose. Despite his nose smelling things in the far distant at that time he still had no idea where exactly this fire was. Forest fire was the worst, it burnt and destroyed until nothing was left, no hiding places, no food. No shelter and no protection. Forest fire meant days of running for cover while it felled trees and fed on leaves and wood.

He slowly slid under the water, taking a deep breath and holding it as he pushed with his powerful thighs, propelling himself far under the water. Fish swam by him but he wasn't looking at them, he wanted to remain hidden from his pack that weren't far from him. The rocks in the other side of the pool were inches from his hand and he reached out and pulled his body toward them, using the shelves to aid his climb up the side of the waterfall. This time though he wanted to do this in secret so he was using the rocks behind the waterfall; the gushing stream of liquid and foam and the roar it made as the water crashed down into the pool was enough to keep his pack from seeing him. Unfortunately it made his journey twice as dangerous. The spray from the water made the rocks to smooth so his hand slipped and he couldn't get a good grip on the rocks. He found that his toes ended up curling over the jagged edges just to keep himself on them and not falling.

The waterfall was literally inches from his back, should it crash on top of him he would be instantly overpowered and fall but it wasn't pushing him under, it was distracting. He felt the power at his back and it seemed to create a pressure that pushed him toward the wall of rocks, at the same time though it unbalanced him. The secrecy so that he didn't worry his pack if the threat wasn't aimed at them.

At long last he reached the top and this time he couldn't help but expose himself a little, he needed to climb to the side to avoid being caught under the water as it fell off the ledge. He took the chance. His thighs were bulging at the effort this was costing his body but he hardly noticed it. He had worked harder before. He had suffered more pain than simple exercise burn. He could still remember, to this day, that fateful day when he had taken the knife that almost killed him. Now that had been pain and he had only been seven then. His little body had been far too small for such a large injury. His wolf had been large enough to take it but the effort to stay in wolf form had also been excruciating.

That memory of complete agony was another advantage to him. He would never fall under the pain given to him by an enemy. It was simple; they couldn't hurt him as badly as he had hurt as a child. They couldn't use mind games, he was already broken to pieces in his mind. They could snap their jaws around him and claw at his skin until it wounded him and made him bleed but the large knife to a small body would always remain his biggest physical pain. Not even his father had hurt him that badly. And that was saying something.

When at last he reached the top he swam to land and began to climb the nearest tree. What he saw only made him angrier, more determined. He started to consider something he had not considered at all, not once in eleven years. In the distance was no longer a fire though he saw little sparks every now and then, the fire was being put out and smoke was floating up in the air looking like long lines of white mist filtering up into the clouds.

This was an attack - another in a big long line of them. What had happened had been and was going and someone was cleaning up from the mess created. It was in an area of the forest he didn't usually go to. It was out of his way from what he could see from his perch. He needed to go and scout that area out and see who was affected by this latest attack. What he knew for certain was that his double life was impossible. Tony's death had proved to him that he had to be completely committed to a single path. He had a responsibility now that took precedent over his vigilante ways and that was his pack. He still wanted to do some good for other wolves out there and even humans. He wanted to do something with his life and his skill, protecting the forest had been that, but he had a better purpose now.

This new purpose meant he couldn't do everything on his own. So what better than to team up with four other alphas?

The thought fluttered in his head and as shame crept from the memory of his running away he couldn't let it go. He couldn't stop wondering what it would be like to return to the family that literally brought him up and showed him that the world could also be a safe place. He couldn't stay away from the people who had taught him that been beaten by your father was wrong and who had shown him ways of getting out his anger and his sadness. They had taught him to let go of those hurtful days and he had. And then he had let go of them.

But while they had needed him these last years. For many years actually. He had saved them more than he could remember, he also needed their help if he was to aid other wolves if this wayward, eastern pack was to be brought down. Forest fire were too dangerous to be smelling and not doing anything about. He needed more scouts, he needed more information. Hell he needed an army of wolves to fight this tornado of barbarians that had made his mate a servant.

Tim climbed down from the branch he sat on. He felt strangely hollow. He had put this off for far too long but he had to grow up now. He hadn't been very grown up in all these years even though he thought he had. He had thought that strength and instinct made him an adult but it didn't. What made him an adult was finding this drive to do what was right even if it meant putting pride to one side. He was going to face the demons of his childhood and tell Eveliina all about his past. He needed to make peace with that and once he had told her everything he was going to do one better; he was going to step up and go back home. Go back to his old pack and see the four alphas. He was going to apologise to them for leaving and he was going to ask that they join together. That they create an army and together bring down this very, very large threat on the werewolf population.

He was going to merge his pack with theirs to make five packs into one. Tim had finally become an adult. Now he was worthy of fighting for Ray and Tendra.

CHAPTER 8

" They won't accept me back easily Eveliina. You cannot be with me when I go back."

"Why not? They are your family, they will love to see you again!"

"I betrayed them!" He said. Finally. "I betrayed their trust. I left them."

He didn't expect the tender brush of her fingers but he relished it none the less. She brushed back his hair and wiped away the sweat that coated his forehead.

"Tell me Tim, tell me what haunts you. Why are you trembling?"

"They... they were, everything to me. But... they didn't know me. They only knew from what I had come from."

Her small form suddenly sat down on the floor infront of him. He looked down at her from his position on the edge of the makeshift bed. Her legs folded were under her and she looked up at him waiting patiently. This was his chance to tell her everything so she knew what she was getting involved with. She deserved to know the horrible truth about her mate.

"My father beat me. Tendra was my sister and she stopped him, she took so many beating for me that her body is scarred. She used to tell me to hide because I was so young. I used to hear her screaming. I could hear when she bit down on her fist to stop her cries from being heard. But I always heard them. I used to dream of them. I can still hear them."

It was like he was back in that house. The house that only looked colourful and bright when it was him and Tendra. When his father was in it seemed dark, grey and dismal. It became a cage, a prison when their father was there. When their father was gone it was a run down but cosy home. He was back in the darkened house now, "I was seven when Tendra found Ray. He was alpha and her mate and he found her being beaten and he saved her and me. Ashton pulled me from under the bed. That was where I used to hide with my teddy bear. I was pathetic Eveliina! I coward in the dark! I let my sister take the pain that was meant for me. And if it wasn't meant for me I still made no effort to save her as she did me! I am a terrible person. I am... unworthy."

He was grateful his mate stayed silent. Nothing she said would have made this any better, any easier. Her silence was blessing as he relived his curse. "But there was a pack that was killing others and had followed us. It ended up killing some of Ray's pack. Ashton never left me. He and Ray became like fathers to me. In the end Ray had connections, when I was captured with Tendra Ray came to save us with three other packs."

He paused, breathing deep. "Tendra was crying, Ray and his men were outnumbered. Ashton looked to be dying. I had had enough. I was seven years old and I wanted nothing more than to cower under my bed again. But I couldn't and suddenly I was angry. Not at the enemy, at myself. I was done with being so little and weak and silly. I wanted to be someone. I heard Tendra sob and it broke me. I felt it make my insides tear and it hurt me. I felt actual pain when I heard her. When I knew we were all going to die all I could think about was that I had never even tried to save

Tendra. Then I noticed that I was getting bigger. I stretching and it felt good. It felt like a relief and I enjoyed the feeling even though it was weird. I changed into a wolf that day Eveliina, I was seven years old and I changed into a wolf, took part in the fight and in the end took a knife for Lebon, one of the alpha's Ray merged packs with. We survived and I was carried back. I was a lost cause for a few days but I lived. Lived to tell the tale."

And that was where things started to suffocate him.

"But after that is was different. I had to go back to a happy family life. I was enrolled into school and I was shown how real families lived. I enjoyed being loved. But I was an adult; I had the mind of an adult, I couldn't play the games of my school piers I was too analytical. I needed to win, I saw it as a challenge whereas they saw it as fun. I was stronger, faster, bigger than everyone else for I already had the wolf with me. So I made no friends. I had only Lewis. Tendra had a baby, Christopher and I swore to my nephew that I would never leave him. That I would protect him. So I trained every day, every night, I learnt languages, I learnt academics years in advance of my own year group. I lifted weights, I went on runs. I did everything to become a powerful warrior wolf and every year I asked Ray to let me be in his guards. I was ready. But they shunned me. They did not see me for the wolf I was."

Only now did he understand his arrogance. But he had felt as if he couldn't breathe at the time. If only he had been more patient. "I saw things no one else did. Our packs were being targeted. So I started to guard the safe-house our four packs lived in harmony at. I ran my own patrols all the while I begged and begged the warriors to take me on, to train me better. To teach me to be like them and let me in their ranks. But they didn't. They still saw the boy who hid under the bed. That was my punishment for my cowardice. I couldn't protect Tendra so I was not allowed to join the packs. I know that is not what they meant but it felt like mother nature had dealt those cards for me."

"What did you do?"

"I... I ran. I left them all. The packs were attack by a rogue and I killed it. I saw it on my secret patrol. Ray should have seen it, he should have been prepared but he wasn't, so I made sure I was ready for any trouble. At the first sign of trouble I warned that wolf. I always do. That is my mercy, I give them a warning no other would give. But the wolf defied me and went for those I loved. So I killed it. I could not stay then. I knew I could do no good there. I also wanted to do something. I wanted to be a warrior and leaving was the only way to do that. I swore to protect the packs and still every day I go and check on them. I killed a wolf the other day, I have nor forsaken them. But I left them. I broke Tendra's heart; she wanted me to go to university. I defied all four alphas and they put up a good chase for me. Eveliina, what I did was inexcusable. They were my family and they accepted me, they fixed me up when I was dying and they gave me the family I had never had. My running away was... it was, so below the care and attention they had given me."

Tears ran freely down his face. He hadn't realised how much he missed them. Eleven years and all he wanted to do was hold Tendra in his arms. He wanted to hold her tight and tell her he loved her. He wanted to tell Christopher he never really left him. Never stopped thinking about him.

"You protect them." Eveliina said.

"It isn't good enough."

"Maybe they will think so."

"No!" He knew it was not good enough and he didn't want such false hope. He would not accept their kindness anyway. He wanted Ray to punish him badly for what he did. He felt he deserved it. He was not going back to happy families; he was going back to punishment and atonement. He would ask that they work with him for the benefit of others but he did not expect a warm welcome. "You are not to be with me Eveliina. I need to face them on my own first. I do not want you to see me brought low. It would hurt you to see me like that. Believe me, if it was just for my benefit you would be at my side but I cannot hurt you like that."

Her delicate arms wound around his waist and gave him a gentle squeeze. "Oh Tim, you're still shaking."

"I can still remember what I felt as a child."

"Hold me back. Hold me as well, I'm not going anywhere." She should have run from such a dishonourable mate. "I am not ashamed of you Tim, I am giving you permission to touch me. You don't need to hold back. I am still yours."

"You should have left me here to cry at my mistakes."

"I will never leave you. Won't you put your arms around me? I know you want to."

"You are too pure."

A little chuckled emerged. "While I quite like that picture you paint of me it is rather disfigured Tim. I am no angel. I rebelled against my mother so many times it's a miracle she didn't turn me out the house when I was a teen. I was a brat. I am not pure Tim. No one is. So we imperfect people must stick together and help each other."

"What did I do to deserve you?" He mumbled.

"You are a good man Tim. A good man! Now hold me."

His arms wound hesitantly around her shoulders and he stayed unsure for a few minutes before he relaxed. His palms spread wide so he could feel more of her skin. His hands almost covered her back she was so slight. Slowly beneath the warmth of her embrace he stopped his shaking. The dull room that caused him to remember his panic and fear slowly retreated to the back of his mind, the place that usually he had to work himself to exhaustion in his weight room before he reached.

He didn't know how long he held her like for, or how she managed to get him in bed but when he woke the next morning he was lying under the covers, still clothed but with his shoes and socks taken off. He must have inconvenienced Eveliina for she would have had to pull him off her. Like a child he had fallen asleep crying. That only made him feel guilty and inadequate. Would he ever feel up to par for his mate? He doubted it but shook his head.

Eveliina was laid on her side, her back nuzzled into him as she curled in the foetal position facing away from him. Her cold feet touched his thighs, as if she had drifted toward him for heat. He hadn't even provided her with a house let alone a proper bed. What they had was a make shift thing that his pack had borrowed to him. Some had been felling trees and making simple beds with the wood decorating them with lots of woollen blankets for comfort. Last night one of his pack members had given up the comfort of their hiding place for Tim and his mate saying they would stay in the hiding hole of a friend. He was grateful for the privacy and the simple comfort of a make shift bed but it was too cold for his mate. He needed to sort out better provisions for his pack.

He didn't want to wake her up, not yet. He wanted to slip off without telling her so she wouldn't protest again but she was likely to wake up before he made it out. He slid from under the blankets and left her to sleep a little longer while he bathed in the water. It was early out, he hadn't realised just how early but the silence around told him that most of his pack were still sleeping and he took advantage of the silence to frame his opening sentence to

Ray. Whatever he came up with still seemed to sound empty and wrong.

It was the sounds of children that eventually made him get out of the water and pull on clothes over his wet body. They would dry as would his body when he walked under the sun. The laughter of small toddlers and sleepy groans of adults had a wry smile on his face. Time to make a move. Checking once last time on Eveliina he was very surprised to see she hadn't woken up. It was a good thing though. Bending down he placed a very tender kiss on her cheek. She mumbled something in her dreams but her eyes stayed closed.

"I will be back later on." He said. He hoped.

Lauri said nothing as he climbed the waterfall. He had told him his plan the night before and his beta merely nodded at the task at hand, nodding Tim off and turning to get back to running the pack in Tim's absence. He walked to the safe-house. He wasn't in the mood to run today. He felt sick. His belly was unsettled and felt hollow. He could taste bile at the base of his throat and hoped it didn't travel further up. He didn't want to be sick.

He would not go in wolf form either. He was to be as vulnerable as possible so as not to anger Ray to complete extremes. He was dreading seeing Tendra's face. Twice he almost turned back around and walked home in defeat but that was the cowards way out. He was not like that anymore. The familiar trees loomed infront of him. This was it. He saw the outer ring of guards. He didn't feel like slipping past them in secret. He wanted to be dragged in as an outsider would be. He wouldn't go in with the pride of an alpha and he wouldn't let on to Ray that he knew how to get through his new patrol. He didn't really want Ray to know anything of his secret journey's to watch over the packs. Though he had a feeling it might have to be brought up at some point. Either way he was going to go in with no illusions.

The first guard to see him called out a warning to the other guards and within minutes Tim was surrounded with five wolves and three men. He recognised them. And they him. A stunned silence greeted him but he did nothing. He only waited for what would happen next. A friend or even an outsider was usually guided to the alpha with friendly conversation but times were dangerous, anyone you didn't know was a potential enemy and Tim had literally walked away a rogue; they knew no different from that day so he stood infront of them as a rogue.

Finally he had defied his alphas and many would no doubt think he had betrayed his packs, he was not expected to walk in with amiable chit chat. So when a warrior he knew was called Jackson came forward with rope he simply held out his hands without even being told. The rope was tied lose, not enough to chaff him but it did restrain him. It showed him who was in charge here. It meant little. This was a new thing Ray had implemented. He had never know Ray to use this method of bringing unknowns to him before but as he said times were too dangerous to be taking such chances these days.

Three rings of a primary guard Ray had before one got to the safe-house. Tim knew how to get past each one but he only walked through with wolves and men all around him. He saw the sand and gravel in front of him. He heard the clearing of a throat and then the silence that followed. He knew that everyone, every wolf and child in the four packs were now watching him being brought to Ray. He kept his head bowed in shame.

"Alpha." The man in front of him said. The wolf moved to the side to expose Tim to Ray and Tim took a deep breath before looking up to see Ray's face.

Chapter 9

He gazed up at the alpha's face and was shocked to see a stubble there that looked uncared for. Lines edged Ray face that hadn't been there when last Tim had looked. Streaks of grey filtered through his hair as well now and despite him still looking so very powerful and having so much muscle there was an edge of tiredness to his body that Tim had not seen on him before.

Ray's eyes flashed and that tiredness disappeared, he looked stern, he looked furious. The lines on his face only added to that effect. Tim would have coward as a child at that face and he expect Ray to reach out and slap him or physically reprimand him in some way. He didn't look the alpha in the eye but he looked at the way Ray had drawn himself up as if ready to burst with anger. His face was red.

The grey coat that he wore was all that Tim was prepared to look at for now as the shame burned through him and he kept his head bowed low. Ray's footsteps were loud on the gravel; the tiny stones crunching and giving way under his feet. He didn't dare close his eyes but he wanted to as his father figure came to stand directly in front of him. Surely Ray would hurt him now.

Hands gently took hold of Tim's wrists, rubbed lightly under the rope to bring a little relief to his hands even though they were not chaffed yet. After a minute of untying the knot Ray freed his hands and stood back.

"How often have you bled for us Tim?"

The question caught him off guard. "What?" He whispered.

"I saw the wolf; it was killed the same way another wolf had been killed eleven years ago. Your blood was on the floor, I would remember the smell of your blood forever Tim. I was around enough of it when you were growing up."

"Your pack is being targeted."

"I had gathered that. How often have you saved us?"

He was actually hesitant to tell Ray, he wanted to keep it a secret but Ray had poured the alpha command into his voice and despite being an alpha himself Tim felt compelled to answer. He didn't want to fight the command either. He wanted to show utter respect for Ray.

"I have never missed a day in protecting you. I run patrols every day. You have a reputation amongst rogues because you have not yet been brought down they try to get to your pack. There have been many wolves who have gotten close to the safe house over the years."

He had said it. Finally. He expected to be challenged and for Ray to ask him if he was saying his defences were weak. What he didn't expect was the feel of hands on his upper arms pulling him in toward a torso. Before he had managed to figure it out his head was resting on a very broad and muscled chest while thick toned arms locked around him.

"My son, you have finally returned home. We wondered if you would ever forgive us."

"What?"

"I shunned you. We all suppressed your desire and abilities as much as we could. We thought you deserved a childhood but we were blind to the fact that you had lost that chance long ago and you needed to be an adult. I am so sorry."

"..."

"Tendra will cry when she sees you. She will damn near strangle you; you know how she will throw herself at you and hug you."

"I left you. I defied you. I turned away from you."

"Because we left you no choice. It is a burden we shall bear forever. But you have proved your worth Alpha Tim. I feel and sense the power all around you. Your shameful face has not taken that edge away from you. You have grown more than I ever thought you would."

He did tower over Ray when stood to his straightest. He had forgotten the crowd that had gathered around. Lebon was still the holding the arm of a lady he was trying to steady as he pushed past her to see him. The panic on Lebon's face was a little puzzling. It was as though he was rushing to see Tim before he disappeared again. He couldn't help but stare at the alpha he had saved as a child, apart from that day they had never really spoken much except when Lebon thanked him publicly. Now though Lebon was walking forward his eyes wide and sparkling, as if he couldn't quite believe that Tim was back.

"Tim." The alpha said walking forward.

"Lebon."

"Why do you look so sad?"

"It was hard to come back."

"I imagine it would be, we did not treat you right."

"Lebon you treated me fine. All of you treated me brilliantly, accepted me as family. It is me, I betrayed you all by running away. I am so sorry I left."

A leather bound arm came forward and clasped Tim's own forearm. "You have nothing to be sorry for." Lebon suddenly fell to his knees infront of Tim. "You saved my life and I owe you a debt. When you told me all those many years ago that you wanted nothing in return I swore to repay you in time. You earned my respect and loyalty that day Tim but instead of showing you that respect I ignored you. I did not train you as you asked of me. The only thing you ever asked me I declined. When you left I knew I had failed you, I never thought I would have the chance to see you again and apologise for my own actions. It is not you Tim who has to be sorry... it is me."

He had no idea what to do. He stared down at Lebon for a minute wondering how to get out of this situation before he deciding to hold out his hand for the alpha to take it and stand up again. It was then he noticed the crowd was not all full of welcoming smiles. He saw some were frowning at him, some looking down right offended that he had returned. He surprised himself by relaxing immediately. Anger was what he was expecting and he could deal with that.

"We don't want you back here!" One woman shouted from the crowd.

"You left your pack you cannot return to it!" Another cried out to him.

"We do fine without you, go back to where you have been these last years!"

"We knelt to you when you were a child and you have forsaken us since. We will not accept you back!"

Men and women erupted around in an angry tirade against him and Ray 's face only got more angry. His red face turning a purple colour that had Tim a little worried for the Alpha.

"Ray?"

"You are welcome back Tim, as Alpha of my own pack me and mine welcome you into our fold once again."

Lebon nodded in respect to Tim, "As do my pack and I."

"We are of Myco's pack. We do not!" A man yelled out.

"Aliysha will not welcome you back either!" Tim looked to Ray,

"This was what I expected more than your apologises. What of Myco and Aliysha?" He explained.

Ray turned to face Tim ignoring the wolves; they would be dealt with later. "Walk with me." He began to lead Tim away from the people and the guards that had bound his hands angering Ray in the first place. Lebon followed.

"For one, the wolf who called out Aliysha's name knows nothing. He was part of Myco's pack not Ali's." Lebon was quick to admit.

"They have gone scouting." Ray filled in. "We found the body you left behind Tim and we upped out guard but yesterday a fire was started and was quickly distinguished to the west of here. It is interesting because it was stopped before it got a hold of the forest. That means there were people or wolves there to stop it before it escalated. Myco has gone to see who lives so close to us and yet has not identified themselves to us as a pack. Aliysha went with him but Aliysha follows a different path in his life Tim."

"What do you mean?"

"His pack is called the Cicatrices pack. That is Latin for scars for they are wounded and scarred rogues."

"I know of their origin."

"Well, they are able to part shift, to remain in the form of a human but utilise the strength and size of wolves so they increase in size - muscle mass and lengthwise. They are trying to use that to their advantage and bring down this pack from the east. We rarely see Aliysha and his men but they come back here wounded often."

"You are worried about them."

"Very."

They were quiet as they left the enclosure of the safe-house grounds and entered the forest. It smelt of freedom.

"You know my men are skilled Tim?" Lebon suddenly asked.

"I do, they pretended to be the enemy for so long I know they had skills that other wolves wouldn't even dream about. Scouts and jesters is what your pack is made up of Lebon." He chuckled a little, as much as that was true it was hardly a great compliment for the abilities his unique pack had.

"Well Tommy sees everything. My best scout he is. He has never told us where you were but the minute you left he followed you. He has reported back to us every week that you are doing fine, sometimes by mouth sometimes in his poor handwriting."

"Handwriting?"

"He watched over you as you watched over us. He is busy most of the time, touching down here only a few days every few months. He is working with rogues and trying to gather information about this eastern pack. As our best scout he is the only one whom I trust to get information on such a terrible enemy. He made sure we knew you were alright."

"Is he around?"

He was hopeful yet a little irked at the same time. If Tommy had watched over him why had he never approached him? Tim had felt so alone and a friend would have been more than welcome.

"He has not been back for a month now. Hopefully he will return soon. It is hard to know that one of my pack is in danger and out there alone but I know he is capable."

"Yeah, when I became alpha only yesterday I realised how it felt. You feel protective over every member don't you?" Tim laughed a little. He was still finding that strange.

"Congratulations Tim. Tommy told us you were landing on your feet, hearing the words, 'when I became alpha' makes us very proud."

Tim looked up into Ray's eyes for the first. Not as a challenge, it was hopeful, it was... asking for reassurance, begging almost. Ray smiled at him in retune, that pride was there for Tim and it warmed him like nothing else had. He had thought it would be so much worse coming back but now he realised that if Ray was his friend then no one else mattered. Except Tendra and Christopher's reactions of course. But the other wolves didn't matter. He could live with their hostility but his family's would break him. And so far he didn't only have Ray, he had Lebon as well.

"I met my mate. I didn't want her to come with me as I didn't know the reception that would greet me but her name is Eveliina, I would love for you to meet her some time. And I have much I wish to discuss with you regarding what I do now and what I hope to do."

"Come to dinner Tim." Ray clapped a hand on his shoulder, "and tell us everything."

CHAPTER 10

He smelt dinner before he saw it. The smell of meat on a spit was strong and the scent of herbs made his belly grumble. The corridors of the safe house were pristine white and very bright. Different. He looked to Ray who was smiling.

"I had complaints that it was too dark. So I made it as bright as possible. Now it looks…"

"Clinical." Tim said wiping his hand along the bare wall. "It's all clean, like hospitals."

"Yes, it wasn't the effect I was going for.

Tim laughed aloud and caused some woman, who were walking past, to turn and stare at him. When they recognised him their stares carried on.

"Nothing to see ladies, go on." Ray called to them hurrying them off. "Four packs are hard to control by the way, the young boys try to encourage rivalry but as alphas we discourage it greatly. We want a peace amongst us that… is proving hard when we can feel ourselves becoming barricaded in our own safety net."

"You feel the pressure of the Wayward pack?"

"I know they are taking over many other packs. We hear many things here as well. I worry that we'll end up with a battle, right on our door step and this safe house Tim was made for one pack only."

The very real threat was shining in Rays eyes. The realisation that if the time came for it, four packs would be trying to cram into too small a space. It would result in chaos, the rivalry of young boys would become the undoing of them - if they took it too far in their panic to survive and get into the safe zone.

"But this was designed with a way out. Passages leading to open space and other land, right?"

"And what land out there Tim is not being taken over? If we go down the passages and evacuate all the packs, what is telling us there will be safety at the end of it? Nothing."

"...You are slowly becoming trapped. You are undone by your own safety. This is all you have."

He started to panic. He hadn't thought about it. He hadn't thought that the house was too small for so many; that they couldn't get to safety. That he had never as a child been allowed down the exist passages and now he had no idea where they came out.

"Where do they lead? I am well travelled, I can tell you where is safe and where is not."

"I can show you the maps."

"You must."

"Where are you based Tim? How much danger is your pack in?"

It chaffed at him to be asked about the safety of his pack, as if he hadn't already thought about it. But that annoyance was instinctual and he pushed it down quickly. This was a friendly conversation and he would not have his wolf instincts ruin his new found friendship.

"We are by a waterfall. The rocks hold lots of hiding places and the water makes the boulders slippery. My pack are well practised at climbing about the rocks and used to hiding in the caves it provides. We have a constant look out. My pack is made up of Rogues. Lots of rogues who didn't want to be in that position. They were seeking sanctuary. I gave them one."

"They turned to you as an alpha?"

"The most extraordinary thing in the world happened. I offered them a place of relative safety. The waterfall had the water they needed while I brought food. The ground was fertile enough to grow other things. I ran patrols there every day and made sure to check up on them all. It was a resting stop, a temporary safe place until they figured out where they wanted to go. I said I would watch over the waterfall as long as they wanted to stay, but they slowly built up a community until I led rogues there because I knew it had become a family of sorts. I told the rogues they could go or stay as they pleased. Make it their home if they wanted. Turns out they were waiting for me to realise that not only had I created a pack but they wanted me to trust them as they did me. When Eveliina came along I hurried her to their safety and in doing so I gave my 'pack' the most precious thing I had. It sealed the fate and hours later I was an alpha."

Ray nodded to him. "We missed so much of your growing. I guess that time will never be given back to us, but you must fill us in on your life. As much as you can."

"I will." He stopped in his tracks. He could hear Tendra. His eyes started to water without his permission. Oh god this was too much for him. His beautiful sister. After everything she had done for him, he walked away from her. He couldn't go in. But this internal torment was apt punishment. He had to go in. Needed to. But he didn't want to. "I can't."

"Tim?"

"I can't go in. I can't do it, I'm sorry. Oh my god," he pushed passed Lebon, ran away from Ray and sprinted for the door. His heart was pounding in his chest, he had come back for her but now he couldn't do it. He couldn't face the shame. What a coward he was! He wanted to stop and tell her how sorry he was. The sounds of beatings echoed in his head. Her screams and cries of pain, her whispers of comfort to him. Everything she had sacrificed and he had dared to walk away from her! He should not have come back. He should never have left in the first place. He was a terrible person. A coward through and through, even to this very day as an Alpha. He was nothing but a little boy hiding under the bed.

"Take one more step Tim and I will personally pin you to the floor."

He halted again. Her voice. She sounded angry. She had every right to be. He refused to turn and face her, instead keeping his eyes closed not fully aware that tears were streaming down his face.

"I worried about you every day. From the moment you were born, to this very day when you are running away from me now. Don't you dare run away from me Tim. Not from me."

The anger in her voice made him squeeze his eyes closed. How he longed to fall on his knees and huddled into himself. He was vaguely aware of the odd person walking around trying to get to dinner or to various places of their home. He was walking into a packs very daily life.

"I didn't... I did. It's just... I." Nothing could justify his actions.

"You needed to be free. You needed to be the wolf you weren't allowed to be here. I know Tim. I understand. It still hurts." A gentle hand was on his shoulder and he felt the pressure trying to turn him around. To face her, but that last sentence to him had been spoken while filled with sadness. And he found that worse than the anger. If it were possible.

"I'm so so sorry. I ran away and feared you. I didn't want to come back in case you shunned me. So I stayed away longer.

"You idiot! I would never shun you." A sharp hit across his bicep had him turning abruptly to Tendra eying up her raised hand. "Doesn't mean I'm not going to hit you for leaving me!" she hit his arm again but he saw the smile on her face. He would never hurt her back and her slaps could barely be felt across his muscles.

"Tendra."

"Oh, Tim." She threw her arms around him and squeezed him with all her might. The hug hurt worse than her slap but it was comforting to have her hold him once more. Her thin frame still towered over him. She had been given the tall gene while he got the muscle gene.

In the middle of the hallway they held each other and wept at the sight of each other again. For all the time they had missed spending with each other, it suddenly felt as if they had never been apart when they hugged and laughed and cried together.

He felt when Tendra tensed up and knew instantly who had seen the scene and who was last to be faced. He closed his eyes again. His Nephew; who was more like his younger brother.

"I won't hug you. Or welcome you back." Came his cold voice. "You left me, you promised that you would always be there for me but you weren't. I trusted you Tim and you left us. I won't welcome you back."

"You play football well!"

It was a desperate call. He yelled after Christopher as the young man was walking away. "I watched you! Everyday! I've seen you play football I've seen every one of your birthday and Christmas presents. I wanted to send you one but I couldn't bear it if you threw it away. I saw in the blue shirt last Tuesday. In your new football shoes the week before. I saw you when you pierced your ear, I saw you friend with the long black hair pierce it. I watched."

Christopher stopped halfway down the hall but he didn't turn around. "I left you but I watched over you!" Christopher carried on walking. It didn't matter.

"Watching isn't the same as being there Tim. It would have been nice to have an older brother to guide me during my teen years. But you weren't around."

Tim watched him walk away. Not all homecomings could be as happy as others. He was aware of Tendra leading him away from the corridor he stood in and towards the smell of food. It didn't smell as tantalising as it had before. He wasn't as hungry as he used to be. He wanted to walk away and come back tomorrow maybe, today he felt like he had outstayed his welcome but Tendra was talking in his ear and picking up a pate, leading him to the buffet styled dinner that was laid.

Ray said nothing at all the while they got their food and sat back down. Great mounds of food covered his plate and he wasn't used to having so much in one sitting. His life was as fugally lived as possible. He stretched his money out to the last penny and grew most of his food. He also shared everything with his pack and knew that money was better spent on provisions, in case of emergency, and not for mountain styled plates. It was good however to eat his way through most of it. His childhood appetite was coming back to him.

"How do you live?" Lebon asked.

"I was a part time mechanic and I built my own house in the middle of the forest. I go to the waterfall every day to wash and that was how I scouted out the place as safe for my pack."

"Was a mechanic?"

Ray suddenly joined back into the conversation and Tim put down the meat that was in his hands. "The wayward pack killed my boss. They were warning me that I am a target. Yet, one they will not find so easy to bring down. My mate also is wanted by them. She knows what they do to the packs they take. She was a slave to them."

"More information?"

"Yes, but I don't think its information we need right now. I think it preparations for war. It is inevitable. We just needed to ensure safe passage for the non-fighters."

"Where is that though Tim? Everywhere is dangerous these days. Even guests in my pack are not treated to a warm welcome as they would once have been."

"I know. I had no intention of having a pack Ray. I did not want to lead. I was content with the status of a rogue; one who fought for others but was a lone wolf none the less. I do not yet know the abilities of my pack. I have not tested or asked my beta about them but I have toddlers in my pack."

"Can you bring your pack over to here?"

"I will not risk that. You have four packs already and room only for one. No."

He put aside his plate. "The land between my pack and yours is not taken though it is open. An attack could happen. I still don't know how many of this enemy pack there are."

"Tommy might know. The Cicatrices may know as well."

"Whoever knows we need to move quickly Ray. A fire near here is not a good sign. I need to get back to my pack tonight but I will come again tomorrow."

"Tim!" Tendra suddenly grabbed his arm in a powerful hold. "Don't leave us again."

"I won't. I promise. I came back because you're all in danger. You did not let me as a teen but will you let me know, eleven years later – fight with you? Protect you?... Be a warrior for you?"

He fell to one knee and placed a hand over his heart – it was an old gesture but the meaning was strong. He looked up at Ray and Lebon who were watching him with shocked faces.

"Of course. It is an honour to have you fight alongside us." Ray reached down and clasped his hand bringing him to a standing position once again.

"Thank you, I will make you proud. I will earn all four packs trust again. Now, I need to know what I am dealing with; show me your maps, I needed to see where your exists come out at. I want a count of all your pack members, separate figures for warriors, children and non-fighters. I need a list of your food store and a tour of your entire compound here. I need to see where the other packs live."

He was straight down to business and while Ray was tempted to bristle at the sudden command and takeover of leadership, he had to acknowledge that Tim had more experience and knowledge of this situation. "I will take you through it all."

He led Tim away from Tendra and through the eagerly listening pack ignoring all and talking about the logistics of his safe house. None of them realised that Christopher was stood in the shadows listening and watching Tim.

CHAPTER 11

In the end he had to make his way back to his pack and to Eveliina. The figures didn't look too good. If the packs became surrounded and blockaded in, their food stores wouldn't last for very long. The passages to 'safety' led to open fields about six miles away and while currently they were safe ,Tim had no idea how long that would remain so.

The land itself around the safe house and the various buildings that housed the rest of the pack, and the other three, was surrounded with gravel for added security but it didn't help with the situation of food. The fire to their west had created a ring of devastation; as short lived as it had been, trees fell quickly in dry forests. There was no one around either, no wolf nor human that seemed to have been the ones to have put the fire out. Tim suspected rogues had been staying there and quickly stopped the fire but fled soon after to safer ground.

The issue of rogues was a terrible one; Ray had reported seeing more and more of them and Tim himself was no stranger to their vast number, nor their reluctance to be rogues. He had sworn to fight for his old pack but had one of his own. Commitments that he was bound to keep were piling up but he wasn't so sure how it would all work out. He was eager to bring Eveliina to his family, his old pack and not only show her off to them and introduce her but show off his family to her. In short he wanted each to get along with the other and the hostility from his nephew and certain members of the various packs meant he didn't want his pack going near them. Not yet. He wanted to proof himself first, prove himself as a friend, not a betrayer.

Ray was adamant that Tim had become who he was today because of his hard decision and his continual guarding of his old pack, and merged three, was an admirable quality to his name. Tim agreed with both sides. He had tried to remain loyal and honourable with his old connections but he also knew what a betrayal he had caused. The ground he covered between Ray and others and his own pack was too vast to expect pack members to travel across easily.

The danger was everywhere and while he had spent years feeling it increasing, years of feeling the hairs on his arms standing to attention, he knew that now he was thrust into the very middle of it. Something he hadn't opened his eyes to. Silly as he had been.

He was sprinting back, eager now to speak with his beta and get some advice that wasn't bias. The edges of the forest were thinning out, his waterfall coming closer and closer. He smelt it then. The terrible odour of the wayward pack and he knew before he saw anything that the worst had occurred. He didn't have a chance to see it. A blinding pain cut into his back and he screamed in agony at its burn.

The scream at the back of his throat turned gruff. His vocal chords changed to that of a wolf's growl and his eyes turned. Once round coloured irises lengthened and thinned to oval, yellow slits that glared out from his face. The muscles in his body were pulsing, pumping and he felt his form start to change into a wolf.

But at the same time he saw the blood pooling on the ground underneath him. He should not have been changing, he should have been far too weak to do such a thing but he had always known his body was designed for endurance and fighting. There was no giving into the human side, not anymore. He would die here.

But he would not die on his own.

His teeth lengthened and he let loose one more growl. One of warning. He never did attack without that warning. It was his small mercy. Those who stood before him now were those willing and prepared to fight for their own cause. All others would have run off.

He saw their faces amongst the trees. Two males and many more wolves. Their faces may have been half hidden, their mouths that of a snout but he knew a smirk when he saw it. And he returned it with one of his own. He wasn't the first to lunge forward. Neither had he completely changed into wolf form. His legs were still human legs when the wolf infront of him rushed forward and knocked him backwards. Giant teeth punctured the flesh at his neck and dug in deep; he howled in pain and anger as they sank in and held tight. He was not foolish enough to shake his head either, that would only tear his skin that bit more.

He felt the heavy weight of his opponent and he tried to push up but his body shook with the effort, he was laying in his own blood and he was getting weaker by the second. Still he had not gone rogue only to die so easily.

With his hands that were not paws he flexed his claws before looking for the soft spot of the wolf on top of him. He sank his claws deep and held on as best his could. The back legs of the wolf started to scrap at his own, trying to get to his belly, but he felt his own legs change. He was wholly wolf and now he was a force to be reckoned with. Wounded or not, he would not die like this.

Breathing deep he pushed himself up from the floor, taking the weight of the wolf that was on his belly. He rolled over and felt the skin rip at his neck, the blood spurted out and down his fur, coating it in the sticky substance. He felt a little sick when he saw it run down his shoulder and mingle with the white of his fur. Still he pulled at his neck and snapped his jaws. Pulling at his hands he ripped his claws upward pulling with them tufts of fur and lots of blood.

The wolf under him pushed up and tried to roll him under again but he was too quick for that. Hastily putting a leg out he sank his claws into the ground and held on until the wolf stood up. And then he knew he was in for in. Six wolves lunged for him. One landed on his back and he struggled to stay up. Another attacked his legs. One went for his face. His original opponent was stood by watching and the other three were circling him, wondering when it was going to be their turn to attack. He felt one of them go for his flank and he tried to stay on his feet when their added weight and biting teeth pulled him down.

He kicked out his legs and hit the wolf in the mouth. Whipping his head around he narrowly avoided a biting again. Then he whipped his head back and knocked into another wolf sending it fly to the side.

The waterfall was so close and his pack either could be in danger, or could be wounded from damage already done. His worry for them increased until his heart was beating loudly in his chest for their safety. He didn't know what to do. Lifting his head he did the only thing he could think of - he made a call. A desperate call; not for help or aid, that was not on his mind, it was call of an Alpha to a beta. A call with which required only one howl back to assure him his pack was safe. Just one howl.

Another wolf jumped on top of him and his legs went from under him. Collapsing in a heap he looked up with bleary eyes at the sky above him. One howl and he would let them take him. Let them kill him because fighting was getting him nowhere. Until then he kicked out his leg and furiously lunged forwards, using his teeth to bite anything that came too close.

Like a cornered animal he managed to maintain a distance from most of them due to his pure venomous anger. He eyed them up, as they gathered in a waiting circle around him. All ready to pounce. He saw one of the wolves, a light brown coloured one step towards him and he lost it; leaping towards him he sank his teeth at the neck and swung his head sharply to the right. Blood spurted out but he carried on shaking his head, desperate to kill the wolf infront of him. All the while he was aware that there was no howling. No reply. His pack was wounded and he couldn't get to them.

Another wolf was coming at him sideways, aiming for his soft belly and he turned quickly to meet that wolf but only to have the angry claw of another sink into his back. He leaned backwards, fiercely growling and pulling his body away. The claws were ripped from his back as he moved and he caught the lunging wolf in his jaws, right on the nose. He clamped down hard and heard a whine. That was when he knew he was doing some damage and he looked at the wolf caught in his teeth. It was barley an adult. The minute he started to show such mercy though the wolf flung out his claws and scratched along his belly so blood beaded up in stripes. He bit down harder and harder on its nose and then in a quick movement, when he sensed another coming at him, he swung his head to the right and back to the left. Snatching up the wolf's throat he bit harshly into the windpipe until the second wolf lay dead at his feet.

The two in human form came out, guns in their hands. So that had been the blinding pain at his back. Wolves had used mortal means to hurt him. There was no honour left in this pack. That was the lowest of the low. Wolves had weapons enough, they did not need, nor was it acceptable to go using human weapons as well. It was cowardly. Battle was done hand to hand or by such weapons that required hands to wield them. Bullets were wielded by metal, the skill was in pulling a trigger and guns took away that physical strength that was part of training. They took away fair opportunity. That was the worst weapon of them all. He snarled at the men but he was surrounded. His pack not answering his call.

His eyes began to shut, he was too weak for this and slowly giving up. Tendra's voice in his mind was saying, "it will all be over soon." It rang loudly. He heard it from all those years ago when she told him he would not have to listen to her pain much longer. A wolf lunged and fell on him again; his legs gave way instantly and he felt the ground. Another piled on top as his mind wandered to his sister. Another blocked his head and another at his back. The men came forward with guns in their hands. He couldn't move, he was pinned.

"It will all be over, just you wait and see." Tendra's smile seemed to be infront of his very face but he knew she was miles back, safe in a house that had a safe exist... for now.

But it wouldn't be safe in a few more weeks. The house wasn't all that safe anyway it turned out. His felt the pressure and heard the click from guns but he was frowning under the heavy weight of wolves. Tendra was not safe and neither was Christopher who he had promised never to abandon. Did giving up to death class as abandoning them? Surely he should be fighting to save them now? Especially since his own pack were more than likely dead after such an attack. Or maybe they weren't. Maybe they needed him and he was laying on the ground accepting his death?!

Anger blossomed inside of him as he heard the click... then the bang. The gun was let off...

... he pushed up from the floor, his limbs shaking terribly but his determination was twice fold what it had been when he first felt he bullet in his back. Now he was wide eyed and struggling but he lifted up the weight and felt no bullet pierce him, though he heard them hit flesh. A howl told him that another wolf had taken his bullets. He pushed up more and with gritted teeth that drew blood he lurched the wolves from his body. Running swiftly to the left he avoided another bullet but it grazed his side giving him yet another wound. He was too outnumbered but he wouldn't give up so easily. He looked around to see another wolf dead on the floor. It was the one that had taken his bullets.

He looked towards the men, this would be a daring task. He began to run, not in a straight line, in a zig zagged pattern towards them and even as they shot their guns they ran out of bullets. He didn't not give them time to reload as he jumped and landed on them both sending them to the floor. With his claws, he latched onto the throat of one, and with his teeth he locked onto the other.

The two men lay dead in seconds and all the while others were pulling at his tail, biting at his legs. He turned and snapped at them but they cut viciously at him. He felt his back legs falter and then change. He was fading, changing back to human. His body was giving up. His mind was fighting but his body couldn't do it anymore.

"At least I tried." He told himself. "At least I tried... for my packs." His eyes closed but he stayed standing, stayed trying to see his opponents even when his eyesight was narrowing.

In the distance he saw more human forms. This was it. More backup for his enemies and he would be dead in seconds... But one was not walking straight. He strained his eyes, looking at the oncoming humans. His body was taken a hold of abruptly and flung across the floor so that he landed on his side. He didn't stay down though he stumbled back to his four feet and looked the attack head on. Twisting to the right he avoided another wolf. Still the humans came, a slow walk but it was quickly reaching him. Then he saw who it was. He saw that familiar smirk, the familiar face of a laughing and jovial wolf. A wolf who chose a side and stuck at it with loyalty. This was no enemy; this was someone who had come to help him.

"You're a little late Tommy." He greeted.

"Ah, not that late, you're still talking. Get your ass up, you ain't doing no good on the floor now are you?"

He would have looked offended if he could muster up the strength but a wolf he had never met, nor knew, came and nudged at his body. Slowly it helped Tim to stand while Tommy and his comrades made quick (and loud) work of the wolves that had attacked him. Soon the wolves that had gone for him were being flung to the floor. Tommy himself picked up a gun lying besides the fallen human forms. He looked back at Tim, "If they chose the weapons with which to attack, they chose the weapon with which to die."

He let the gun explode; a bullet whizzed out from its chamber and kill an oncoming wolf.

"So the rules of engagement have changed."

"Lesson one Tim; rules don't exist with packs like this one. Take me to your pack; you have a lot to learn from me. Though I have to say, you've done rather well over the years. You've made me proud!"

Tommy was laughing away as he helped the now human Tim over to the waterfall. Even when he pulled Tim into a fireman's hold, in order that he might help him down the waterfall, he was still muttering about, "Tim not using his eyes."

"What'd you go getting yourself shot in the back for? If you're really lucky I won't tell anyone how careless you had gotten. I'll save that embarrassment for you to carry with my little friends here."

"And who are you're little friends?"

He watched as they easily climbed down the waterfall.

"They are rogues. I took a little lesson from you Tim and I also befriended. Turns out, Ray isn't the only alpha that rogues are making for. These prefer you. I told them I would take them to you. So; you gunna let them join your pack?"

"...Guess my pack just doubled in size."

"Good man. Now stand up before Eveliina screams."

CHAPTER 12

"Oh my god! Tim! What happened? Oh God, you're bleeding badly."

Eveliina came running at him and her hands were instantly running all over his body checking him for wounds, and of them she saw many. If felt like her heart were beating at the back of her throat it was pumping that hard. He had been shot, his neck bitten badly and slash marks bled at his stomach. Not to mention all the other little injuries she saw over his body, especially on his legs.

"I'll be alright Eveliina. Tell me what happened here, is everyone alright? Why did not Lauri howl back when I called?"

"Lauri is wounded but he knew enough to know you were fighting when you made the call. He couldn't answer you and he didn't want another to make the call because it would distract you too much - to know something had happened."

"Foolish idea. I was more distracted waiting for a reply. I needed that call; I needed to know the situation. I thought the pack destroyed!"

Eveliina nodded her head at him aware that, while he sounded angry at Lauri, he was more distressed at knowing his friend was hurt. "How is he?"

"Let me worry about you for a minute. You need to sit down. You're losing too much blood."

"I'll be fine." He went to walk past her but swayed and the world span. If not for Eveliina's hands he would have fallen, as it was he felt himself being lifted up once more by Tommy. For such a small guy Tommy sure did have a lot of strength.

"You need patching up Tim, let me sort out your pack for you. I will report everything to you when you wake. Sleep now."

He couldn't help it. He was drowsy anyway from lack of blood and the minute he knew that there was no pressure on him to stay awake it was like his body had an automatic switch; and it sent him off to sleep in an instant. The last he heard was a lot of commotion as everyone around was muttering that both Alpha and Beta were hurt and new wolves were invading.

"Friends." He called out in his drowsy state. "They are friends. Trust them!" He called to his pack. The muttering stopped at once but then, so did everything else, for he fell unconscious after that.

Eveliina had never felt so worried. She had not even been this worried for her family, and she had been petrified for them. For some reason though it was harder to see him so wounded, the mate bond was very strong. This new guy, who did a lot of crouching and a lot of watching with his head cocked to the side, was looking over at Tim with an unreadable but very concentrated stare. It was one of the new wolves who took off Tim's shirt and assessed all the wounds. He rolled Tim over one way and then the other before calling out for all their supplies.

"Do you know what you are doing?"

"I was training to be a healer in my other pack; I know enough to get him through the night. Tommy has a lot of experience as well, we will watch over your mate." He assured her.

"What has happened here?"

This 'Tommy' asked her the question moving in towards her. His eyes seemed to cut deep inside of her and he had a smile on his face that she was sure was only a distraction. He was eyeing her up very carefully, assessing almost.

"We had just prepared dinner when they came. Thy started to climb down the rocks but this pack are adept climbers. Those who can fight jumped onto the boulders and started to fight. But the water was fast and the rocks slippery. Lauri was overpowered by two wolves and he slipped from the rocks. Brendon caught him and broke his fall but then he too slipped and they fell down. It wasn't as high as Lauri initially fell but it was enough. They're both alive but Lauri is badly hurt. Brendon fell into the water. Lauri didn't."

"The attack was soon over?"

"They saw that we had fighters and they left when they couldn't get any further towards us. But they got a good look at where we live."

Tommy nodded his head. "They must have been watching Tim for a while, but not enough to scout out properly. It was a sloppy attack. So why attack and risk lives? How many was there?"

"About fifteen. At least five were killed and they were washed away down the stream. I didn't watch too carefully, I went to Lauri and Brendon when I saw them fall."

Little drops of blood fell to the floor; she heard them hit the cave floor and her eyes widened in horror. "Tim."

"Don't go worrying about him, I've seen him with much much worse."

"Worse?!" At this Tommy laughed. She was almost grieving at her mate's injuries and this wolf here was laughing. Her anger built rapidly and it must have shown because he held up his hands in surrender and stopped laughing. Though he didn't stop smiling.

"When he was seven years old he turned wolf."

"I know, he told me he had changed young. He told me everything."

"Well, when he saved Lebon from the fatal knife he took the blade himself. Imagine a seven year old with a fatal knife wound ripped through him and then trying to tell him not to change back into human form or the wound would be too big for his small body. He held on for a while but then changed back to a small boy and that, Eveliina, was the worst wound I have ever seen on something that small. So don't you go worrying; Tim will survive this."

At that last word Tommy was squeezing past the rocks to go outside, he just left her, quite suddenly. Shaking her head she watched the other wolf as he was dosing Tim's wounds in alcohol and then sewing them up with a curved needle and thread. She held her stomach hoping she wouldn't be sick. "He can't feel a thing." The stranger wolf said to her.

"I'm sure he will when he wakes."

"Yeah but he's a tough guy. He was doing well against seven. With a bullet wound as well, he proved to still have a lot of strength."

"So who are you."

"One of your pack now, Lady Alpha. But my name is Solomon."

"Pleased to meet you, Solomon." She greeted. She didn't want to make him feel uncomfortable if he was joining the pack and quickly smiled at him in welcome.

In the end she had nothing to do but watch as Tim slept. She didn't know what to do; she herself was not a leader but in Tim's stead she and the Beta were supposed to step up and work together in his place. But the beta was out of action as well. There was only her. It was as she was staring at the moon with her back to Tim that she noticed eyes watching her in the darkness.

"Aargh."

"It's Tommy, Lady Alpha."

She clutched at her heart while he moved to stand in the little pale light that there was. "Don't scare me like that."

"Sorry, I'm a Watcher. People don't see me unless I want them to." She nodded at him and looked back at the moon.

"You are wondering what you can do?"

"Yes. I do not know how to lead a pack. And Lauri is asleep."

"Then let me help you."

She eyed him up. Take the advice of a complete stranger? "You are from one of the packs that Tim used to belong to?"

"He was not from mine but yes. My pack and his merged to form a joint alliance. He knows me. A lot do. I go far." He smirked.

"What do you find funny?"

"Life."

She shook her head and refused to look back at his and his jokes.

"If you don't mind my saying so, your pack cannot stay here. The secrecy of the pack is uncovered. The strength of your hold has been exploited and while the enemy pack retreated, they go with more information than they had. They know where and how you live. They know your defences... and lack off. They will return with more adept climbers. Fighters more than you will be able to count will soon descend the rocks and you will not be able to defend yourselves. This was a scouting mission Eveliina; they will come back for the slaughter next time."

"Then where do we go?"

"Follow the water."

The water was flowing fast; the lake led off to somewhere they had not explored. Everything they needed was in this enclosure and they had simply stayed where they knew it to be safe. She didn't know whether to trust this stranger, especially when he was telling her pack to go into the unknown. How did she know that the wayward pack were not waiting for them?

"You lived under their rule did you not?" Tommy asked swiftly.

"Yes."

"It is not something you want to go back to, is it?"

"No."

Her voice was but a whisper. "I don't want to do anything without Tim's say so."

"Tim will not be going with you darling. You are a leader here. You and the beta will have to team up in Tim's absence."

"What?! No I am not leaving him!"

"Keep your voice down or you will wake everyone up and those kids didn't want to sleep in the first place. Gave me a right headache they did with their whining."

There was little else to say. "What do you mean; really mean, tell me what it is you are planning."

"Tim is needed elsewhere. He needs to fight. His pack need protecting. You can follow the stream and enter a different forest. One where the wayward wolves don't dare to go."

"Why will they not go?"

"Because that forest is overrun with rogues."

That glint was in his eyes again. Tommy had done an awful lot of scouting. He was weary to the bone but his rest would come at the end. He smiled at her. "Tim has made a right name for himself. A wolf who gives shelter and food for as long as needed; protection as well, all free of charge. He asks for a little information if they have it but has never pushed for it. Your mate has become a rather well known wolf in parts. As a protector of the rogues. So when they want to join a pack they want to go to him, when they hear of his name. But they do not always know where he is located. Many rogues gathered together in that forest and they defend it as best they can."

"Are they not a pack now?"

"No, they have no Alpha - they wait for the 'right' one to come and lead them."

"But you said Tim wasn't going with me."

"He isn't, there is no need; I brought the warriors with me."

He nodded up to the top of all the rocks, to the top of the water and she saw figures. Lots and lots of figures stood by the rim of their home watching over them and the land around.

"A guide will take you to the forest where there are many rogues left to protect you. The rest will go with the warriors of this pack and go to war with the wayward pack."

"You planned this. Tim has no idea?"

"Tim has no idea but as for planning it, I merely put the pieces together that Tim himself created. His name is being whispered throughout the wolf world darling. Everyone needs a protector when times get dark. Everyone needs to hope for a strong leader who will lead them into the light. Tim has become that person, and that means he has secured protection for his pack and warriors to help him fulfil the promises he has given to others."

"When he wakes-;"

"He will try to beat me to a pulp for not coming and seeing him in all these years. But I can't very well be a Watcher if I don't take enough time to observe things."

"You are rather cunning Tommy. And I think this is a good idea."

"Good; because you are going at first light."

CHapTer 13

She was all packed. Having no belongings meant that she had nothing to take except provisions but they were stored in wicker baskets and various backpacks. Everyone who was going carried at least one pack. Most of the rogue warriors had descended and now those who were the guides and protectors, of their little bunch of non-fighters, were ready and waiting to set off and take them to safety.

Rebekah stood next to her and the few children that were part of the pack were stood solemnly by. Most had opted to stay behind but Brendon had been told that he had to go. Despite his arguing he had eventually agreed. He was still young and they wanted to keep him as innocent as possible.

"Besides we may need you to protect us." Eveliina had said. She knew it would pain Tim if he had to take him with him into a battle but Tim would have done had the situation arose. Eveliina wouldn't and she made sure the situation did not arise. Only Tommy was stood by eyeing the lad up and assessing him. She glanced Tommy but he immediately put on a smiling face when he saw her looking at him. "You leave that boy alone." She said when Brendon was out of earshot.

"Of course. " But he sounded too... pleasing for her to take him seriously.

She had said good bye to Tim but he was still unconscious and had no idea she was going. She plucked a flower from the ground and left it by his head so when he woke up he would know she said goodbye. It felt wrong to leave him in such a way; with no word to him, when the sun was only just rising and had not yet cast light in the sky. She had to step up though and take care of the pack and that meant that those who couldn't fight needed to go. They had to get somewhere there was less likely to be war. She cupped his cheek in her hand. "Goodbye Tim. Come back to me at the end, I'm waiting for you. Don't leave me." She whispered into his ear.

Gently she reached down and placed her lips over his, feeling the softness there and lingering for a second. He was too injured to even wake at her kiss and it was with a heavy heart that she pulled away. She stroked back his hair once before sharply turning and leaving him lying on a makeshift bed with the covers to his chest. It made him look slightly more vulnerable than usual.

"I love you."

He knew instantly when he woke up that something was wrong. Not only was it too quiet at the waterfall for such a time of the day (the sun was shining strongly and it seeped into the cave he was in) but Eveliina wasn't there with him.

The sound of children was absent, the rushing water all he could hear. By his head there was a little flower and he felt a little tingling in his lips that made him reach up to touch them. But nothing was there. His back hurt a lot, it burned a little when he moved and it was hard to move at all. The claw cuts stung and his neck felt as open as it had been last night but he felt the stitches and knew it to be closed.

"You look like hell."

"Feel it too."

Tommy was stood in the doorway, his arms folded across his chest and one leg draped over the other as he stood leaning on the rocks.

"Where is Eveliina."

"Safe."

"That doesn't tell me anything. Tell me plainly, Tommy."

"I sent her off with some rogues to follow the water to the safety of a certain forest I know."

Tim was up, out of bed and walking toward tommy with a look nothing less than murderous anger. The pain of his wounds were long forgotten now. "You sent my mate away!" He was about to swing for Tommy when the man, twice his age and half his height, held out one arm and stopped Tim's swing before he had even raised his hand. "Don't make an enemy out of me, I've done you a good turn. You needed your pack protecting and I sent them to the safest place I know of. I sent them to the rogues that will soon be part of your pack."

He did not let go of Tim's arm, instead he pulled him outside to where the sun blinded him for a minute. Slowly Tim was forced to get used to the sun and eventually became aware that a lot of strangers were on his land. "Who are all these."

"Rogues who wish to join your pack. Assuming you have already said yes; they agree to go with you to Ray and fight in the war that will rage between you five packs and the 'wayward pack' as you have taken to calling them."

"What?"

"Yes, sit down, you're swaying a little."

Tim sat, almost collapsed onto the floor as he looked at the many men all around him. He recognised a few of them as part of his own but most were new faces.

"They have waited in the forest a long time hoping to meet you one day. They want you to be their alpha but regardless of that, they will help you now to protect Tendra and the other packs."

"What of Eveliina though."

"I told you she is safe. Now then in two days we go to Ray's. I have already sent word ahead to get all the non-fighters from all four packs into the passages that lead to the hills. At the hills are more of you pack – well new members of your pack - waiting to protect them. So no need to worry about that bit either."

"You mean these rogues are waiting at the hills?"

"New members of your pack, yes. Get used to it."

He looked around at the warriors of his 'pack' and couldn't believe how many he had. "There are lots."

"Yes, the wayward pack has done quite a number on most of this area. As you can imagine the number of rogues forced to flee, either because their packs were enslaved or slaughtered, has increased dramatically. There are many rogues in that forest I told you about. I won't tell you now, you're white with shock, but you have a very big pack."

"I'm missing half my blood that's why I'm white! Not shock." Let him have some pride left, since everything else had been taken care of while he slept. Urgh he felt terrible and now he was hastily trying to fill himself in with the schedule.

There was only one problem. "How do you know there will be a battle?"

"Ah, that's the bit where I give you permission to hit me." He stuck his tongue out at Tim and hoped he would take this lightly. "I was doing some... scouting... with a difference."

"Explain."

"If I saw them do something bad, I killed them."

"Essentially not the biggest problem. But go on."

"Well I got myself caught didn't I? They set me up. Innocent little kid got killed because they were trying to lure me out. I'll never forget that... but anyway, I fight well. I had already set up the safe places and for the rogues to join in and all the others things so... well... I just..."

"You set up a battle didn't you?"

"What was I supposed to do? They were coming for you all anyway. I'd listened enough to hear that they were planning an attack as soon as they figured out your weak spots. They were already getting geared up to go to Lebon, Ray, Myco and Aliysha. You were next after them. You're a warrior Tim, the merged packs needed you there. And you needed the threat to your own pack eliminating. I just set the date on our terms. I gave us enough time to prepare - otherwise they would have come at you all in surprise. I did what I could to save everyone."

"And they let you go?"

"When I promised I would be in the battle... Then I slipped my hands out the handcuffs and ran. Literally ran away from them."

Tim looked around at his pack home.

"We had best be on our way then."

CHAPTER 14

Two days later and Tommy agreed that Tim was fit enough to go to Ray's. Before then he had insisted on Tim staying in bed no matter what but time was ticking down and they need to get there soon.

The run to Ray's was actually quite nice; it had been two days since he had done any real exercise and while he still was not recovered as well as he would have like, he was better. He had healed quicker because of his wolf but it would still be about three weeks before he was completely healed. The stretching of his legs brought with it a feeling of relief to his muscles. He stayed behind Tommy who was leading their company. Tommy's crouched run looked comical at first until the actual logic of it came into play. Squatting almost to the floor such a run was nimble and quick. Tommy refused to go into his wolf form; he was more agile as a human. He peered round corners before he took them with his body and he was low to the floor to avoid any initial attacks.

His bent knees worked easily and he could dodge surprisingly quickly, running off to one direction with little warning. He was a springy little thing as well who was jumping over fallen tree boughs before Tim had even spotted them laying in the way.

Before long, following such a quick guide, they were at the edge of Ray's domain and they were not greeted like friends.

"Tommy you return but with a traitor and a horde of rogues. What is the meaning of this?!"

"Go and get my Alpha Lebon and Alpha Ray. They will let us enter."

"No, we do not believe you and do not want to get into trouble for disturbing them for trivial matters."

Tommy immediately cocked his head to the side. "Trivial matters? War and allies are 'trivial' are they? What has gotten into you Jir? That you would turn away friends? Let us past now."

"No. Be gone with you."

"You know us to be here legitimately or you would have bound our hands and taken us to the Alphas, why do you hinder us."

"We do what is good for the alphas... even if they do not see it themselves."

"Let us through!"

"Enough Tommy." Tim put a hand on his shoulder to calm him. "If we are not needed nor wanted then we shall of course leave. Come on."

Tim had to literally drag his rather strong friend away from the guards; Tommy was all for fighting them till they were unconscious and then reporting them to the Alphas.

"Hush Tommy, I know how to get past their guards. It's rather easy if you are any good at timing."

"What."

"How do you think I got past them to guard my family?"

"It's isn't about ability, of course there is a way, it's principle Tim! They are disobeying their Alphas, putting innocents in danger and it leads me to wonder if my messenger got through to tell

Ray to send the non-fighters through the passages, while there was still time."

"Well the latter depends on who you sent. For now let's wait a half hour then slip past them. We can greet Ray with surprise and quickly announce the situation."

"So close to battle Tim, a split pack is too dangerous. If we can't work together how can we be expected to fight together? There's too many enemies on a battle field without putting our kin in the mix as well."

"Agreed and I have to say that is my fault. I do not blame them. I left."

Tommy stopped dead in his tracks and turned to face him. "And I watched you become a very lonely person who worked weights because it was all he had. You made your decision and stuck to it. They did not help you while you were there, those who turn from you now are the ones who ignored you as a teen begging to be taught. So what you, went away so what? You did not sell anyone out. You brought no enemies down on them. You left peacefully, you watched over them and you return peacefully announcing your help in their safety. Hell Tim, you didn't kill anyone, or cause a catastrophe. You went on holiday for a while so you could 'find yourself'. Get over it, they have to."

Tommy himself was walking away shaking his head and muttering about childishness but whether that was directed at Tim or the obstinate guards Tim never did know. Right now that didn't matter; he was busy explaining the timing to the new members of his pack.

"Alpha Ray!" Tommy yelled across the entire gravelled ground earning the stares of many of the warrior wolves. "Next time you want allies, tell you're guards to let them through. We just had to sneak past them. Not very good those guards."

Well that broke the tense atmosphere. And brought another with it straight away - Ray look furious. Lebon came forward half turning wolf and it was only when Myco restrained Aliysha did the packs understand how strong this information was. "If you cannot accept my son back into the fold then leave it! He is here to fight for you and your family! Leave now and don't look back if you will not follow my orders regarding him. I need no rebellion amongst my pack!"

He spoke with a venom in his voice that scared even Tim. He had never heard Ray speak like that and it warmed him inside to think it was for him. Still this was the first time he had seen Myco and Aliysha and he eyed them up. It was only when Aliysha came forward (his body far too tall and his muscles bulging) and gathered him up into a crushing bear hug did he know everything was fine between all alphas.

"Ah, I've missed you Tim! It hasn't been as fun since my cute teddy bear wasn't around to squish in big half creature hugs."

"Thanks Aliysha but I'm grown now. My muscles are too solid to hug this tight, you're popping me."

Myco hugged him next and Tendra was at the door; waiting for him to go to her this time. He wasted not a minute. A gathering was ordered straight away, all warrior, guards, alphas and kin that had stayed behind were called to the centre and told of the plan.

"When do they attack?!" Someone shouted from the crowd.

"We have maybe two weeks, maybe less." Tommy answered.

"How are they armed?"

"They come with human weapons. With guns. They have rope, and hammers. Axe's and knives. This will be a bloody battle."

"We need weapons!"

"Who protects our children?"

"Are they well trained?"

"Do we have any hope?!"

"Enough!"

Myco stepped forward. "As for hope, as long as we fight for what is right; and that is the protection of our pack, there is hope. Of course they are well trained, the rumours of all the fallen packs is evidence of their skill. This will be a hard battle and should you choose to walk away from it then you can. But it will go ahead. It must. It isn't just our pack affected by them! There are many."

"And more are coming to help us." Tommy put in softly.

"What?"

"Yeah sorry Tim, this is just a few rogues out of the many ... that.... there...are, yeah. You're a big alpha."

Warning. All he wanted some warning from his friend but no, he was getting surprised every step of the way. "More, I have more?"

"Well do you want to live through this or not? Your rogues are trained at least."

"Warning would have been nice. What of Eveliina."

"There's plenty left to look after her and your pack. Don't worry about them, they are totally safe. As for Brendon, he'll be fine as well. Eveliina just panics."

"What?!"

"Ah... I didn't tell you that bit did I?"

"No, but you're going to."

"He was my messenger."

Best to tell Tim before he finds out from Tendra his young friend came to get the children out. As it was Tommy was taking great pleasure in seeing Tim's face slowly turning a shade of purple that was as comical as it was shocking.

"You sent a young boy out with the task of getting here unharmed, past hostile guards and a wayward pack?!"

"I'm sending him to the safety of the hills with more of your new pack to protect him. He wanted to protect children anyway. Now he can have an active role while in relative safety."

"Diplomatically put Tommy. Without my consent! It does not happen again!"

"Of course not. For now... Ray, your guards are too hostile, they need moving if our pack is to get here. As for weapons, Tim owns a garage."

"I do?"

"Oh, did I tell you I know your boss?"

He was going to burst. Like water bursting from a river dam. "Go, on." He said tersely determined to hear Tommy out before he punched him.

"Well, I watched you for years. I saw you get a job at a nice garage and I liked the sound of your boss's voice. So I went to the same café as him, got a coffee, asked him for a glance at the morning paper and before you know it, Tim, you had introduced me to a good friend. I liked the guy. Shed a tear at his funeral. Well, burial whatever you call that beautiful thing you did."

"And me being the owner comes in where?"

"Well, I always knew he liked you, didn't take much to convince him to give it to you when he retired, or in his will should he die before."

"You're unbelievable."

"I'm practical. You lived in a hut and didn't have much money. Besides, think of all the tools we can now go and get and bring back to use in a fight. You got lots of hammers in that place."

If he thought his day was going to get any worse , at that moment the rest of his 'new pack members' came strolling in as if they had been invited to afternoon tea for the sixth time in a row.

"Alpha." They greeted him, piling in amongst the crowd of warriors already there. Five packs all mingled together did look rather impressive; they were bursting out of the compound. Needless to say that as more came and nodded to Tim as their alpha, the respect from the four packs seemed to increase. The hostility died down and the threat of attack started to force logic into everyone's mind. Tim was bringing back up – willing or not, planned by him or by tommy (or by any other out there conspiring behind his back) or not. Tim was now a leader and a powerful one at that. His pack was rivalling, in size, at least three of the packs already here and Tommy had said the rest were split into groups protecting others. Allies of Tim were plenty. He didn't look quite the big bad wolf any more.

All this time Ray had been silent, silently hiding his amusement at Tommy scheming and Tim's shocked and angered face. It wasn't everyday he saw his stoic brother in law/son (the bond was too close to differentiate blood and bond) looking a little faint with information overload.

"Well, let's get dinner on shall we." He announced. "We can organise a weapons gathering session tomorrow, for now, let's get everyone settled in and counted. That would be a start."

"If they all fit in the dining room." Tim mumbled turning away from Tommy, still shaking his head.

CHAPTER 15

His new pack members looked rather wild. Their hair was long, neck length and messed up in tangles that looked as if a comb would simply get stuck there. Their clothes were worn and dirty but looked durable. And they wore boots. They all were carefully looking around the dining room, testing the food a little bit before shovelling great mouthfuls down as if they hadn't eaten in a while. Yet they were all big men, they must have been eating fairly well to keep the muscles as big as they were but then again Tim was assessing his own wolf. Sometimes instinct was more prominent than actual health. He would have to question them on that, already thinking of their health.

He wondered at their names, and how on earth he would remember them all. His older pack members were eying up the new additions with slight trepidation and intrigue. He was pleased they weren't fighting with each other but then again they had all been forced to go rogue so maybe they would bond very well. He felt the bond of an alpha over his pack in the new members already. Acceptance had brought about swift consequences and he was drawn to the newer members; he wanted to talk with them and get to know them and assess their abilities. There would be plenty of time to get to know their abilities in the coming weeks though so he wasn't overly worried about that bit.

He ate his own meal sat with Tendra, Ray, Myco, Aliysha and of course Lebon. The alphas all together must have looked impressive; as the biggest of all the wolves they were the most threatening in any form. And Tim really had filled out in the years of isolation. Those who knew him from before still could not believe how big he had gotten and that innocent teenager asking for training now seemed a rather distant memory.

"Where is Christopher?"

"He wouldn't come in while Tim was here." Myco said lifting the spoon to his lips, "Sorry Tim. You have your work cut out there."

"I expected it, it's alright."

The truth was stark and he glanced around the room, mostly the wolves around were eating happily and chatting away but as he looked around he did notice the hate filled glances of others. Seems he had some making up to. As it was the wolves were crushing into the dining room, some sat in groups on the floor, other crammed on benches around tables and more yet stood in the corners or by the walls just trying to be in the room and eat. Some had even grabbed huge platefuls and left because there simply wasn't enough space.

"I built my own house by the way," He started. "If you ever need any help in building extra room for the packs let me know. I'm handy with tools."

"At the end of this we may take you up on that offer. The compound is filled with many houses for but this is the safest house and we really could do with extending it."

Tim himself was thinking about the tools in his garage and debating with himself. Tommy was under the impression that they could use his tools as weapons. He on the other hand was sickened at the brutality that would insight. Hammers and screw-drivers had no place on a battlefield. He was an honourable wolf and it sent shivers through his very blood and bones to hear such talk.

"I may own a garage but I don't want the use of tools on the battlefield."

"Your mercy Tim will not be shown by those that come at you." Was Ray's answer. Tommy hurriedly came over to them and sat down after eavesdropping.

"It won't. Best to have back ups." He said settling on a chair.

"It's barbaric." Tim persisted.

Myco put down his spoon and looked up at him. "The battle you saw as a child Tim was a coward's battle as well. They carried whips and chains and rope. Lebon's pack can wield choice weapons as well. That is what we must do now; the enemy love their wolf form but they want extra, they want to be able to feel that power in human form as well."

"Then we must remain honourable and fight in wolf form, we must put aside the humanity in us for we are not human. If they chose to fight us in human form then let them but we can do more as beasts than we can with make shift weapons we have no idea how to skilfully handle. I hit a hammer as well as any but faced with a knife I have no idea what to do first. Or which would break in a battle of strength. We should use what is naturally given to us. We should protect our keep with the principles we intend to instil into our children."

"We would be under equipped!" Aliysha interjected.

"Under equipped? Aliysha, you and your pack are not under equipped; you are half beast half human, they do not know that. Your pack offers a power and strength that the rest of us cannot imagine. Lebon - your pack are not skilled in warfare but in tactic and cunning. They are our weapons in this."

"And if we start to lose?"

"What good will it be if we try to reach for things we cannot use anyway. They have guns Ray. Guns. Hammers and a full toolbox of instruments we can use to hit people with are little protection against guns. We cannot fight in human form against guns, a bullet wound to a human is serious, a bullet wound to a wolf is bearable. We can take more bullets in wolf form. So we need to utilise that."

"Guns are cowardly!" Ashton burst in.

Where he had come from Tim had no idea but he sat down now besides him and looked furious at the mention of them. "If I kill, it will be with my own hand, not the cold metal of a death machine."

"And that should be the mind frame we have on the weapons." Tim agreed tentatively. He had yet to see Ashton again and he was wondering at Ashton's reaction to his return. The man gave nothing away though. Ashton was an uncle to him and Tim was ashamed to see him so abruptly and talking of war not peace.

"So what do we do in the meantime? What do we do to prepare for this war?" Aliysha said.

Tim who was still looking around the room knew what had to be done. He assessed everyone; some liked him, others hated him. Some saw him a child, others as a warrior. Some thought him a protector and many thought him a leader... best to step up to everyone of those things.

"We train together; we show each other our strengths and weakness. We put our trust in everyone here and created a merger. We become one pack fighting together and to do that requires trust. Showing each other our weakness will not be easy but unless we do, we do not know how to utilise our strengths."

He too had now put his spoon and pushed away his plate. For those who didn't like him, tough, he was leading now.

"We have Tommy's knowledge from his scouting, we have mine from my rogues and I am sure once we share everything we will come out with a little picture of what our enemy will be like. We train together for two weeks and learn well what will be our defence."

"Our attack." Lebon muttered.

"No. We defend." Tim raised his voice, spoke up and looked Lebon straight in the eye. A dangerous thing to do with an Alpha and he saw the snarl build at the back of Lebon's throat. "Yes I disagree with you. You may want to attack but we need defence here. We are not wholly animals. We have the ability to kill and that should not be used so lightly. We must let them come to us first. For honours sake, and because, defence has better strategy."

The glean in his eye told Lebon that he had a plan. "In defence we can lead some away from the battle of strength. Using your people Lebon I intend to feign weakness. Tommy, your walk itself is a good thing to use. You do not walk straight, and for any that does not know the reason why, it looks to be a disadvantage. Aliysha your pack I want hidden until revealed at the end. The shock of seeing such creatures may make them pause. Me and my pack are climbers, we have to be as we live in a waterfall, we can station ourselves on the buildings and overlook the battle field, taking down opponents when we are least likely to be seen and most likely to be used. My new members are rogues, used to defending the forest and little else I am imagining - but I need to see them train. They can be part of the front line defence. As can yours Ray. If we utilise skills like that we lead them to their downfall. We are prepared for whatever move they chose to make. Defence to its upmost."

There was silence around the table for a good few minutes. No one spoke as they all seemed to be taking in what he had said. He wondered if he was offending them by taking over but he didn't care, he had left some of his pack to fulfil his promise here, he would be an active member. Still the silence dragged on... until,

"Best get training then." Ray stood up and carried his plate to the kitchen area calling for his pack to join him when they were done.

"Well done Tim, you're making a fine leader." Tommy whispered into his ear.

Chapter 16

Rebellion was inevitable. Some claimed that Tim only wanted their weakness exposed so he himself could take over the packs. It was whispered – rather loudly – that he was going to bring down the alphas and rule them all because he was part of the wayward pack. Some even went as far as changing into wolves and charging at him; to which he let them pin him to the ground. He let them wound him and he watched as Myco or Aliysha took control over their own packs. To fight back would be to show them he was a threat. It would take away the opportunity for Myco or Aliysha, or even Ray, to discipline their packs and so would reaffirm this suspicion that Tim was trying to take over.

So it was with great calmness that Tim was hurled to the floor day after day, spoken over, glared at and had insults thrown at him. He bore it with a patient that had Tendra walking away. She could not bear his indifferent expression or see him willingly get hurt. All the alphas knew he was capable of doing great damage to those who attacked him. Everyone knew, but those who hated him used his peaceful nature against him knowing they could get away with it.

The sense of family had long since gone and even within a single pack there were quarrels and arguments. Only Tim's pack remained tight. His new and old members had merged into a community and they took turns in walking around after him. They would be there to protect him if ever one of the other alphas weren't not there to take charge of their subordinates. The dedication of his pack was startling to behold. He hadn't ever felt like this before. Tim found that he was immensely proud of them and their skills, and the smallest accomplishment; even just one of the youngest climbing one story higher than he had previously, felt like his own child had achieved a great prize. Being Alpha came with a lot of benefits, it felt like he was an over protective, happy and proud father.

His own pack's fighters were good but while he led them in exercises to improve their strength and taught them some martial arts to improve flexibility, in human form he referred them to Lebon for human fighting techniques. It ended up turning into a circuit around the compound, with Lebon doing hand to hand combat training, Myco doing wolf form fighting, Tim improving the physical human body while Ray focused on strategy and Aliysha began attempting to teach others to do what he and his pack could do; that part was however proving a little futile. It seemed the Cicatrices pack were completely unique brought together by their horrific experiences and so in the end Aliysha concentrated more on the training of his own pack for their own ability. All credit to him though he didn't give up on those that had shown some initial progress.

The compound itself was rigged for battle, always had been, and while it had been improved for comfort since the merge, there was very little to do to strengthen their already robust stronghold. Tendra trained with some of the other women, the men wouldn't fight them properly insisting they would not hit a woman but they were trained in fighting none the less. They did their own fighting and Tim had insisted they focus on their wolf forms as that would be their strongest. There were only a few females wolves left and they were actually very good. He was surprised; having never seen females fight he was rather shocked that they too could be so brutal. He was never getting on the wrong side of what seemed like beautiful and graceful women. Their grace only made it harder to knock them to the ground. He had tried, for a laugh, and while he checked his punches before they made contact he spent a good while trying to get the female he was competing against, to the ground. He was just as pleased with their skill as he was with the men but he was always aware of those who did not come to his training area of the circuit. The rebellious wolves did not join in with him working together on their own. They even talked when he began telling them of his plans.

It would not help in the long run if they had a split defence but he was preparing for that eventuality as well. He had been in quiet, whispered talks with the alphas on what to do should their packs divide. The Alphas were furious, almost beyond angry, at the members. They threatened to send them away, to banish them from the pack and make them either rogue or forced to find another pack they were more inclined to obey. Tim stopped their harsh punishment though.

"Not so close to battle; to send them away is only to send them to their deaths. Focus on that after we are all saved." He had said. He would not make his way back home and find the dead bodies of those who had opposed him on the way. Needless to say that the smirking Tommy had been sat crossed legged on the floor when he said in a reedy sort of voice that they did not deserve his mercy before he stood up and made to go over to one of the disobedient wolves. Tim, used to Tommy's abrupt ways by now, had grabbed his arm and forced his bread roll into Tommy's hand.

"Ah I knew you wasn't planning on finishing that." Tommy then sat back down with one leg pulled up and began eating. It was lucky that Tommy was so easily distracted.

Tim had not met Christopher at all since the first day and when he asked the Alphas had not either. "I'm worried; if he is not training he may not be prepared for the attack."

"He won't go down the passages, he wouldn't go to the safety of the fields and leave us." Tendra told him with her eyes glistening. To see her brother and her only son at an impasse was hard for her. She knew it would take time but in the meantime it felt as though her own alliance was divided and she was eager to please both. Tim told her to concentrate on her son but she couldn't let Tim out of her sight. Too much had happened in the past to separate Tim and Tendra and yet the bond between mother and child was just as strong. Tommy had told Tim in secret that he had heard Tendra crying to Ray at night, that she didn't know what to do and that she didn't want to leave her room in the mornings because it would all start again. She didn't want her son to hate her.

The food was going down rapidly with the new additions adding strain to their stores. Tim didn't know if it was worth leaving the compound so close to battle for more stores. Tommy had said no and that for Tim had been the final word. The Alphas still tried to persuade him but he took the word of Tommy very seriously. It was no evident that Tommy knew more and planned more than anyone else around, to clarify that reasoning Tim only had to looked at his own pack. Tommy had panned it all and so now his word was not to be ignored lightly.

With a week left until the battle was due a sense of tension hung in the air. Worry was starting to make them more agitated and in the end a party of about ten wolves went out to go and buy some more food. Tim protested loudly and Tommy agreed but the hostile pack members were quick to discredit Tim again and in the end, to put an end to the shouting match that had occurred, Ray sent out those ten to find more food. He argued that the battle might take longer than planned, or that they might become locked in their own compound. It was a given that they would not be going to the safety of the fields, not only would they not lose their homes but it was about time the wayward pack were taken down.

The hunters did not come back. No more food came to them and everyone worried about what had happened to the ten that had gone. It was a hard few days after that; expecting their warriors to return and knowing they weren't likely to. Those that had protested Tim's words no longer looked him in the eye and he wasn't pinned to the floor half as often after that. While harsh words weren't spoken to him now he was still avoided by those who didn't like him. While it was an improvement in many ways he still didn't like it. They knew his words now held some validity to them but weren't willing to back down from their hatred.

The most surprising thing happened when there was only one maybe two days left until the battle; Tommy sent on four men.

"What are you doing?!"

"Using your reputation again."

"What?"

"Never you mind Tim, all will be revealed now go back to your bicep curls."

Completely dismissed Tim walked away, Tommy may not have been his alpha but he wasn't stupid enough to go against Tommy's words.

"You and my Tommy sure are making good friends between you both." Lebon said walking forward.

"Your Tommy is playing me like a bloody cello. He's up to something again and it has to do with me. He just sent out wolves from your pack to somewhere I have no idea."

"Tommy... always was my little mystery. He came to me the very day I thought of the plan to take down my brother. He seemed to know my plans before I did and he was always the one to get information. He is my scout, Watcher, he calls it but I know enough to trust him with my life and the lives of my pack. They know him enough as well, he has their safety at heart. Go with the flow Tim, I do." Lebon clapped him on the shoulder and looked over at Tommy for a second pondering. "He never did tell me his past. Or how he came to walk like that. As far as I know, I think he is incapable for standing up straight."

"Really?"

"Oh yeah, I've never seen him with a straight back. Springy little thing he is. He reminds me of a frog, try and catch him and he will just leap away. Don't tell him I used a frog though, his wolf would feel rather belittled."

Tim was laughing quietly to himself as he looked back at Tommy, he had never seen the guy use weights, or fight hand to hand; Tommy wandered off during the day and it was a curiosity because Tommy had carried him down the waterfall when he had been hurt so he was strong and skilled but he never saw the guy train.

The men that Tommy sent out did not return either. Steven, Joe, Lucas and Eicca were the four Tommy sent out and no word came back as to where they were. Tommy only smiled when it was reported that they weren't to be seen and when asked about where they went, he seemed to go temporarily deaf. So when the sound of a distant horn could be heard blowing through the forest they were mighty worried about all fourteen men sent out. The time had come though; that was no musical instrument designed for songs, that was the sound of a warning. War had come upon them and all five packs scurried around getting into position.

Aliysha and pack were behind all the buildings. They were to be hidden until the last minute and used when the enemy had been lured to the back of the buildings. It was an extra comfort to know that if the buildings were knocked down then they had one last defence. Myco was at the front of the gates - his pack the frontline. Tim and his climbers were on top of the buildings watching the trees in the distance as they seemed to sway with the approaching pack. Everyone else was scattered strategically on the gravel, the rest of his pack that did not climb stood at the base of the buildings ready to catch any that jumped off to get somewhere quickly. It was all set up.

The horn was getting closer and closer until it wasn't just the sound Tim heard, he saw the heads of humans walking through the trees. He saw wolves, many many wolves all coming at them. The gates at the front of the compound were manned; it had been a while since they had needed to be closed so forcefully and finally. Tim was trying to count how many they were to fight when his eyes widened to near bursting.

He couldn't let himself worry about numbers, he changed quickly into his wolf form and jumped up on his hind legs, calling out a warning to the approaching company. It was one long howl, gruff and fierce and it barked out the mercy Tim always showed. They were used to the call, he had used it on many of them in his past eleven years. He let his body change back to human form and called out to them. Well, yell out was more like it, he was not at the front of the compound and they were on the other side of the gates.

"Leave now!" He called, "Or you won't have the chance again!"

A chorus of laughter followed his words and they continued to march on towards the gates. Tim nodded, "So be it." Changing back to wolf form he took his place again in the middle of the roof he was stood on. He was aware of the stares he was getting of most of the packs but Tommy sniggered, "He always gives a warning. Then if they come at him, their death is their own fault. He told them." Ray nodded, his majestic form tense and ready to pounce in an instant. He glanced back up at Tim who looked down at him. He didn't like to attack. He had experienced too much pain as a child to enjoy inflicting it others as an adult. The understanding went between them; wolf eye to wolf eye but they understood one another.

That stopped mattering any more though because a second later there was a metallic bang on the gate and it lurched. They were beating the gate to get in...and it soon fell.

CHAPTER 17

When the gates fell they knew the strength of the wayward pack was too much. It was as if their nerves all pulsed at once. This would be a bloody battle and they were sure it would not end well. Tim had seen the numbers from the forest as they had surrounded the compound. Five joined packs had meant a few hundred warriors all were ready and waiting to defend but they were defending against double their number. And it wasn't just the growls of wolves he heard but the beating of drums, the thudding footsteps of human feet and the cracking of metal chains being swung to hit the ground with deadly strength. A gun blast went off just behind the gate and from his position Tim could see many, many wolves in human bodies; he assumed each of them would be carrying a gun. They had no armour, no bullet proof vests. Nothing against such fatal pellets.

They had known guns were in the mix but had thought their wolf forms enough, as the vast number of opponents crept around and circled them, blocked them in, they knew there were going to be too many bullets whizzing in the air. Tranquilizer guns were at the ready in some of the human's hand and that scared Tim more than anything else. This was not just a kill mission. They wanted prisoners at the end.

He looked around at all his rooftop comrades to see their eyes were wide in horror. They looked afraid. Scared. Grown men scared.

"It's going to be alright."

"They want slaves." Tommy called up to him. "They are creating an elite. A new world; one that werewolves rule. They take slaves to build their new empire; once the wolves are dominant they will slaughter the humans one by one and have fun doing it."

"You knew this?! You hid this detail from us?!"

"I hide many things that are not easy to take in. They want a race of the strongest wolves. The strongest here will be taken back as prisoners; they will test them, breed them, research on them, all to see what makes them the strongest and by that create a breed of wolf that will have no difficulty in wiping out the humans."

"Why? Why such a grudge against the humans?"

"They are tired of staying secret from them. They are tired of knowing that if humans found us, they would experiment or exterminate us. So they seek to do the same to the humans before it can be done to them."

He watched the enemy walk forward, coming too close to the warriors. "What now?" Tim yelled to Tommy. "What now?" They were outnumbered in number and in weapons and with terrifying consequences for the prisoners of war.

"We fight to the death."

"That's it?! You get me a business, a pack with numbers I can not even count, you orchestrate a battle then you send my mate to so called safety! You even sent four of your own pack out to certain death. Tommy – what have you got planned?!"

"If I tell you that Tim, it wouldn't be a good plan now would it?"

"I least we would have some hope."

Tommy sank into a deeper crouch, he was about to lurch forward form his position underneath the rooftop that Tim was stood on. His spritely body was slowly uncoiling; his muscles were flexing and twitching. Tim was shocked that such a small body could have such active muscles under his skin. "Tim, I did not lead rogues to you so you could look to me for hope. They are all looking at you. Being a leader is not just planning. It isn't just running away and building yourself up. Being a leader is knowing that you might be the loneliest person in the world but there was a purpose that put you there and you never forget it. Being a leader Tim, is building a hut with no prior knowledge, it's confronting rogues who could kill you. It's leaving behind your family because you hope in doing better. Now, Tim being a leader is putting aside your fear and being the hope to your pack who are terrified at this moment. Don't look at me for fancy words, I'm fighting."

And with that Tommy bounded off jumping through the crowd of frozen warriors towards the fallen gate and finally - right into the middle of the enemy. Tim screamed at such an action. "Oh god no." Tommy, was right in the middle of the enemy, he needed to help him but they had a set strategy. He couldn't leave Tommy to fight for himself but everyone was frozen, hopeless in the face of so many opponents. He looked around, he didn't want to do this but if he didn't, everything he had done would have been for nothing. There really was no choice.

"Men!" He called, "Women!" He turned in a circle to eye up every single one of them; alpha or not. He looked deep into their eyes and saw the stark fear that he knew had been in his own before making the decision. "We may not be many, and we may not have guns but we have honour and families to protect. It may turn out to be our defeat, but we will make sure we do not fall lightly! We are not defeated yet! We fight! We fight to the death! Think of your families, think of your homes. For a better world, for a peaceful world... We defend!"

He let the change take him again as he shouted the last word. He let it echo through the changed vocal chords to transform into that of a majestic growl and when he saw the enemy hacking down the last remnants of the gate Tim let out a howl of rage. Let them come. The wolves all around threw back their heads and called out to the blue sky above. The ones in human forms called out a scream of challenge and when the enemy finally broke free, the lines of Myco's pack sprang into action.

CHAPTER 18

T ommy was lost to Tim but his battle was just as fast paced. Like a swarm of bees the enemies literally oozed into the compound, their feet crunched in the gravel and shouts, screams and growls were instantly heard. They covered the ground and engaged in fights almost immediately. They ran over to the buildings and broke down the doors, many streamed inside the buildings looking for huddled up non-fighters but they had been sent on ahead too long ago to find them now. The passage way had been hidden, covered up and were rather secret.

Not only did they pour into the building but they started to climb up the very outside brick work to get to the roofs. They came up from the side of the buildings, some went slid inside through the windows to check out the higher floors. It was mere minutes later than on top of the very roof, Tim was fighting for his life came enemy wolves. Tim's position had been seen from the start and they intended to bring him down... once and for all.

Drool was sliding down the side of his mouth he was baring his teeth so much. He snapped viciously with his jaws letting the sound of teeth on teeth threaten those that came to him. He wouldn't be taken down easily. He snapped to the right and caught a human leg. He threw himself backwards and pushed a wolf off the roof, grabbing onto the ledge with his paws just in time. His claws cut deep ridges into the rim but he didn't worry about that now, hauling himself back up as teeth lunged for him he jerked his body to the right. The wolf that went for him fell off the roof too and then he faced three humans.

Crouched down low he made to spring forward but one raised a gun at him, pointed it at his face. Ducking his head, he pushed hard with his thighs and bounded forward to charge full speed at the one who held the gun. At last minute he veered to the left and pushed the human to the floor of the roof and used his body to pin him. With his teeth he clamped down the thin neck and crushed it instantly. The sound of a gurgled death was not pleasant but it signalled that Tim could get up and fight the other two.

A sharp sting on his back had him arching a little with pain. Chains had whipped him and he furiously swiped his paw at the arm that held them. His claws drew blood as they ripped at the man skin but the chains were only raised again. A bullet whizzed past his shoulder blade and he felt it's heat. He ran at the man with chains but sharp teeth took hold of his ankle as another wolf came up to his roof. He kicked out his leg and collided with the attacking muzzle, the wolf went down instantly but was also easily replaced by another.

A bullet hit the floor by his foot and he looked down the little greying bullet and then up at the one who aimed the gun. Bad aim he thought smugly before running. His roof was swarming with the humans and the wolves all trying to bring him down, the walls were covered in the crawling forms of both wolves and experienced humans. All trying to get to him, all trying to bring him down. If he stayed there, he would be overrun, the sheer numbers were far too many for a single man. With all his might and strength he ran. His body hit the offending gunman directly in the chest and both were hurled off the rooftop. Keeping a hold of the man Tim used him as his shield as they crashed to the floor three storeys down. The man took the jarring shock of the fall and saved Tim from too much pain.

Stepping off the dead man Tim tested his legs. All were working just fine, now to find Tommy.

The forest was dark and dismal but her guides had been rather cheerful. She looked across at the few that had accompanied her. There were not many that couldn't fight; the two women, the few children and a couple of men. All were looking a little fearful of the forest. "This forest has been deserted many a year now."

"Why?" She asked.

"Tales, rumours." Lauri said. He seemed dubious, as if he didn't want to step one foot inside.

"There is nothing there." One of the newer wolves was saying. "We came to this forest because we knew if no wolf dared go in then we would be safe. It is filled with rogues and nothing more."

"There were tales of diseases." Lauri said.

Eveliina stopped in her tracks and looked to the children.

"Disease?"

"Death." He clarified.

"There is no death or disease in the forest. It was a rumour, only a rumour."

"What would you do if I told you we would go no further? That we do not want to follow the stream anymore."

"I would follow your leadership Lady Alpha. But there is no cover out here and we do not want the enemy to come on us."

"Where did these rumours come from?"

"From me."

She turned back to face the way they were walking and from up the stream came an old wolf in man form. She knew him to be old though he looked not a day over forty. She knew him to be wolf because his body was still muscled like that of a young and fit twenty year old. Not a day's age or wither was on him yet there was an air of tiredness about that made a strong man look a little vulnerable.

"You started the rumours?"

"I needed solitude. In the days of my youth there was a disease that killed my pack, when the disease left and there was only a few of us left we decided that we wanted to stay alone, the grief of losing our family was too great. The rumours that were already going around we encouraged a bit more until the forest was left well alone. And I and my kin lived in harmony for years until they were slaughter on their way back from their wanderings. The pack your mate fights, is the pack I want dead."

"You did not go with the warriors who went to aid Tim." Eveliina said.

"I am too old now; I can do no good in battle. So I offer sanctuary to rogues and now to you who claims them as your pack. Use the forest, and whatever you like but leave me alone."

"Would you not join us?"

"No. I have seen too much death. I will not see any more except my own, when that day comes."

She never found out his name nor did Eveliina ever see this man again but that day taught her the effects death had on people and she worried even more about Tim. Her own pack had lost members in the take over but she did not see the effects, only the new wolves she was made to serve. Her life had changed but grief wasn't something she had seen all that much.

A life led completely alone is not good and she felt for the man who walked away. The forest turned out to be fairly well cared for, it was not overgrown in any way and some foreign flowers had been planted. It seemed he had not completely given over to his grief, instead he had become a caretaker but still, she wondered if he ever did get the urge to leave his self imposed isolation.

She saw the other rogues, they were friendly and scared but they told her they would protect her to their deaths if the time came to it. Almost instantly the waterfall people started to climb the trees and settled amongst the leaves. It seemed they preferred to be in hard to reach places. Everyone else set about making a fire for light and heat, preparations for dinner were started and some went in search of an adequate water supply so they wash and remove the dirt and sweat that had gathered on them from the travel here.

Eveliina who was helping to collect fire wood couldn't help that her thoughts drifted back to Tim.

"Will he be alright?" She asked their guide, Sean.

"Yeah, Will and Tommy will have patched him up and if I've heard right, he won't be easy to take down."

"But he's wounded."

"When you're in that kind of battle Lady Alpha, the one where it's for someone other yourself, you don't feel a thing. The adrenaline is going too fast around your body."

"You've fought in battle?"

"I was the only one left out of my pack. Tommy found me half dead still trying to revive my brother. I've been in battle. I fought to save my brother with half my blood was on the floor. Didn't feel a thing till Tommy pulled me away from him."

So that was the very real reality of battle. Of death. When they came for her pack it hadn't been like that, it had been quick. She had seen death but it hadn't been anyone close to her. She felt the dread settle in the pit of her stomach and she began to climb a tree. Settling amongst the tree trunk with her legs stretched out along a sturdy looking branch she waited. Waited for Tim to come back for her; all the time wondering if she would get the chance to stop waiting.

Mouth after mouth came hurtling after Tim. He was pushed to the ground, rolled over and bitten all over. His back legs felt a little numb, his own muzzle was sluggish and slow to act. He saw wolf after wolf and he had the horrible situation of not knowing if it was one of his or not. He had seen everyone in wolf form the last few weeks. He had counted them, learned their names, tried hard to distinguish between them in their wolf forms but the truth was, that in the chaos that was battle everything was too fast paced to allow him a seconds pause to try and make out certain little markings or blemishes. Every wolf that came to him looked like it was attacking him and he fought back. Each time he prayed to no particular god or gods that he had not hurt one of his own. It was a guilty worry he couldn't shake off.

Someone crashed down onto his back and he snarled and rolled over instantly, pinning the one who had tried to pin him. He opened his mouth and snarled once more, a threatening and rumbling growl. His claws curled, scraped along the wolves chest and cut through fur and hair. He bent down his head and opened his mouth, inches from the throat when he smelled it. He paused and heard a whine. He looked up, this was not an enemy, this was one of Ray's. He hastily rolled off the wolf and nudged him so he got to feet.

It was then that he noticed who exactly it was. It was one who had pinned him in the corridors many a time. An insolent young wolf who followed his friends in their plans because he wanted to be one of them. The silly youngster had come at him battle to even try and challenge him there. Now he was shaking. Quivering like the string of a bow after the arrow had been spent. And Tim couldn't help the sense of satisfaction that blazed in his belly at knowing he had terrified the wolf so much. It looked Tim in the eye before lowering its head in submission, then running away as fast its legs could take him while Tim tried to get over his smug feeling and get his head back in the battle. He was soon cornered again and it was with his claws that he strangled the life of yet another wolf.

CHAPTER 19

Aliysha had not had to wait very patiently for his turn in the fight either. They came towards him jeering, laughing at his weak, weapon-less form and they looked to his pack and sniggered amongst themselves as they ever advanced towards him.

He had the last laugh because in that moment he did the most extraordinary thing amongst the wolf species. He tapped into the wolf instinct of strength and size. He let the bones inside his body grow and lengthen but controlled it so they didn't progress into wolf form but stayed human in shape. His muscles however bulged. Hair sprouted on his arms, not as much as a wolf, but it looked like a layer of hair was coating his body. He grew half his size again until he stood about nine and a half feet tall. He was the tallest but even the smallest of his pack was still almost eight feet. Like little giants the Cicatrices wolves towered over the enemies, stopping them in their tracks for a good few seconds before they realised that they could not turn back and so carried on with their assault.

The Cicatrices had the power to fight on human legs and as they bent down they swung their massive arms; the bulky and heavy muscles collided with any in their way, knocking them down, swiping at the wayward pack and hurling them feet in the air so they landed harshly on the floor. They walked forward a little with a bounce to their steps as their elongated legs tried to both stay human and develop the wolfish bend. They swung their arms and kicked their legs and reached down with their mouths to bite at any exposed flesh with their piercing teeth. They roared like wolves and shouted orders with low, deep and gruff voices – a combination of human vocal cords and the added wolven cords as well.

Soon the sounded of angry enemy wolves was loud around the compound, they hadn't liked their surprise mutant pack and they didn't like having to try and outwit them. Myco back at the entrance was gate was overcome. Front line meant he had barely a minute to himself as he tried to push back to the horde of wolves and men but he was soon surrounded by them on all sides and was forced to constantly turn in circles to catch any attacks.

Myco was never one to love the fight, he had never incited a war but he had unfortunately had to fight at times to protect his pack. He took little pleasure in it but at the same time he was very good. He father had raised him to a strong wolf and determined leader, so now on the front line he was an apt wolf for such a challenge despite him soon realising the compound was overrun with the enemies. He heard the building being beat at and pulled apart as best as possible. He heard cutlery and plates smashing, windows were put through and the steel shutters of the safe house were being ripped from their mechanical holders but they were not having much luck. All around brick was being chipped and the gravel constantly being kicked up, the sharp stones hit out at people, scrapping and scratching at their legs and the small of their backs. It became a hindrance now as the wayward pack picked them up and hurled them around, aiming for eyes and trying to hit them out.

Myco felt claws slid across his back and he turned, roared in anger and snapping his jaws. But it was too late, he felt the searing burning pain of a bullet in his back paw and another on his hind leg. He fell to the right instantly and a whip lashed his back. Another one lashed around his neck, the thong of it resting on his windpipe, the coil was curled around his neck and stayed there. A punishing weight on his back held him to the floor and soon he was pinned, his paws unable to twitch even.

He looked up and glanced about the compound to how the rest of his pack were doing on the front line. He heart beat hard, he saw matted fur not inches from his face. He recognised that beautiful shade of grey, it was dark, bordering on becoming black. He saw crimson pooling underneath the wolf who was one of his. Twisting his head, the coiled whip tightened as he did so, he saw his pack were still fighting, their snarls still sounding loudly around him. He saw another of his own fall and he closed his eyes as a round of bullet were let loose and he saw the twitching of shot wolves. Another wolf fell on top of his back knocking the wind from his lungs and as the whip was pulled harder to choke him, no more air would relieve his empty lungs. He tried to push up with his legs but the lack of air finally got to him and he felt his eyelids closing... For one minute, with blurred eyes and his violently juddering body he thought he saw another familiar face. One he knew very well, too well. He thought for a second he might be saved, that the body belonging to that face would come for him and save him from death but another wolf launched on top of him breaking his left leg and as he growled out a cry the enemy surrounded him, blocking that familiar face from view. It was too late. He could breath, the pain was far too much and he felt his body losing every ounce of strength, going limp. He did not want to die in wolf form. With the last remaining strength he had in his body he let him body make the change and he lay on the floor, the wounds terrible now for his smaller body. The weight of the wolves was also too much for his smaller muscles and it took only seconds before he succumbed to the inevitable...

...Tommy liked to lay low, so low he was almost a snake slithering around the floor. Crouched so small he went for the ankles of the wolves to bring them down and then he pounced. He did not stay in wolf form; it was too bulky for his subtle way of fighting. If they wanted to bring weapons into this battle, if they wanted to shot at him, he would go for them in his best way.

Like the creeping death he had been known as for a long time, he was a strong little thing really and he snagged at the legs, the wolf nearest to him came crashing to the floor and then he pounced. While go he couldn't perform a stable half change like the Cicatrices could what he could do was change incredible quickly. The minute they were down on the floor he began his change to wolf, pierced their neck and changed back before the wolf form had taken over complete. Then like a ghost he slipped on off to the next target.

He was thoroughly 'in the thick of it' as the saying went. Surrounded by lots and lots of wolves he was simply getting stuck into the challenge that it presented. It was one of his most outnumbered fights and he was pressed to be quick and not been seen by the majority but he was going about his business completely oblivious to Tim panicking about his welfare. He didn't even realise when the wolf he had brought down turned out to be Ray's opponent. He wasn't there when the alpha turn to thank him.

Tendra was by what looked like a hut made of stone and she was furious. A bullet had already grazed by her shoulder and the stinging flesh wound was a little distracting. Never the less she put the pain to back of her mind as best as she was able and carried on defending the one house she would not see fall. Not if she had breath left in her.

She protected the nursery. The place that was constantly filled with wolves, all taking various shifts to protect the vulnerable point of the pack, that was the babies. They would range from newborns to young toddlers too young yet for school but older enough to play and be boisterous. She had taken many a turn in the nursery watching over the children. Some mother wolves left their children there over night when they were in need of a reprieve or because they were struggling. It was a sanctuary; one already within a sanctuary and inside there was drawings from all the children pinned onto the wall. Little toys piled high and the cots and small bed were stored in corners. This was a place that represented innocence; it was the reason they fought that day, to keep the children out of harm's way. And Tendra would not see such a cherished place overrun with enemy wolves that would smash anything they came across.

Wolf teeth bite fiercely into her hind leg and without her consent a howl was ripped form her throat. Ruthlessly turning around she attacked the nearest wolf to her legs snapping at them with her jaws and cutting at fur but not making any deep cuts. She saw another wolf about to break the windows and try to get into the nursery. Ignoring the pain she flung herself at its leg to trip it even as various wolves around her were biting at her and trying to find a way to pin her down. With claws and teeth holding her she felt the weight of the wolves weighing down her body but it didn't matter, she allowed the gravity to pull her down as they brought her to her belly. Then she sank her teeth deep in the legs and thrust up her paws claws unsheathed and sliced the underbelly of the wolf clean open. One down, many more to go. Twisted her body she prepared to fight yet another. She had been in worse pain, felt heavier men and she would survive this, as she had her past...

...His belly was bleeding. He already had a partially healed bullet wound and now his body had a few more recent bullets resting inside of him. He was in pain but baring it, his white fur that once had felt soft and thick was saturated in wine coloured deep red blood and now it felt like straw; all dirty and matted, cut up and in some places it fur fell out in little tufts because great claws had ripped at it.

The clouds were darkening but it had yet to rain, the sun had gone down though it still gave off enough light to still consider it daylight. He hadn't seen his sister for a while nor had he found Tommy. Tim had no idea where the other alphas were and he was struggling to tell wolves apart he saw that many of them.

He wanted to help others, to make sure that none needed his help and if they did he was able to give it. But he saw nothing past his own opponents, which were plenty. He was so caught up in his fighting and surviving by the skin of his teeth, that it was with great regret and guilt that he could think of nothing that what wasn't directly in front of him. He was constantly surrounded, his vision was always blurred with numerous snarling wolves and by now his legs were throbbing and aching due to their wounds.

He hadn't heard any of his allied wolves cry yet. Or human cries, and he couldn't see the Cicatrices so he assumed them to still be towards the back of the compound. Everything looked rather bleak and even as he fought he wondered if there would ever be an end to such a bloody war. Mud splashed up and hit him in the face, little specks fell into his eyes and it stung but he did dare close his eyes for fear that he would be attacked in his blindness. So he put up with the stinging.

He saw another wolf leaping in the air ready to pounce on his back and he rolled quickly out of the way. He had thought that was the worst part of the battle, when they were so overrun it was a game of staying alive but he hadn't been prepared of the explosion. He certainly had never expected that the use of small bombs would be being used on the compound. The sound of familiar cries of wolves he knew however, soon told him who wielded that terrible weapon. He also knew that the cries were ones of terrible pain, if not impending death.

Holes were formed in the gravel as relatively sized bombs were aimed at their compound. They weren't big enough to flatten the compound itself but with lots of them all crashing down consistently it was not only loud and distracting, it was deadly in two ways. The bomb killed then the smoke from them clouded up and began hiding opponent and allies alike until it was hard to see where the attackers were coming from and how was attacking who. It could kill three at once and it was three by three that Tim saw wolves change back into humans form, sprawled out on the floor. Even those not instantly kill great wounds made staying in wolf form almost impossible and yet to a human such wounds were too catastrophic to let them live. It was a death sentence anyway it just took longer to implement.

The entire compound was under attack by weapons on a scale he had never even thought of, let alone prepared for. He closed his eyes. Superior numbers were one thing but superior weapons on such a scale was completely another. He looked down to the gravel his toes were buried in. He remembered the first time he had come to the compound and the days that followed. As a young boy he had played in the little stones, buried his feet on many occasions and claimed to be 'stuck' so Tendra would come running out and tickle him for his playfulness. Now he would most likely die on those very stones.

He breathed out. Well enough pondering, he had done too much of that in his life. He couldn't look at the smoke any longer or the people dying. The wounded needed shelter from the battle and no one else seemed to be going in. Taking a running leap he entered the smoke cloud instantly feeling a dead wolf under his paws. Forcing his eyes open even though the smoke irritated them he let go of his wolf form. He couldn't do what needed to be done with bulky clawed digits and not fingers. He felt exposed in human form, only too aware of how weak it was. If a wolf came up to him now in the smoke he was a dead man. Crouching down low and looking at the nearest body he put index and middle finger to the neck and felt for a pulse. There was none.

Constantly looking around himself watching for an attack he was aware that the smoke seemed to have sent the enemy in the opposite direction least they attack themselves. Still he found that a wolf face came running at him and he was forced to change into wolf form. He wasn't the fastest at the change and he bounded away from the attack, ran to the right to complete the change before going back with a snarl and his mouth wide open to ac-knowledge the challenge. Jaw on jaw locked and both pushed hard with their mouth to try and wound the other first but they were locked together, snarling with spittle running down from their opened lips to matt in their own fur. Their teeth were sharp and were slowly cutting into the soft flesh of the mouth, mingling blood with the spittle and still not one of them would give in this posture.

Another bomb went off and Tim felt the ground under his paws shake frantically and then a force seemed to hit him in the chest propelling him backwards until he landed in a heap on the floor. Dazed he turned back to human form and shook his head rubbing at his eyes at the same time to try and make sense of what had happened. His right shin hurt terribly and looking down he saw a lot of blood. He couldn't hear anything either, it was as if everything had been muffled. It was a blessing because all he heard for the last few hours was horrendous snarling, threatening and loud wolf cries that tried to shatter his nerves but failed. On the other hand, not hearing anything in battle was a weakness he didn't want. It was eerie and dangerous and he tried to look around him but everything was white. The smoke was too thick and dense. Well, he would have to feel around then.

He tried to stand but his leg shook once then gave out completely. He would have to sort that in a minute. Feeling another body by his hand he checked for a pulse and felt a faint one. It was thready, faint and close to giving out but he would try to save the wolf anyway. He knew the women were guarding the nursery and it was toward there he would take the man. Sliding his arms under the body the human form shivered and then groaned. Bending further down Tim stared and stared as hard as he could to see who it was in his arms. His heart lurched harshly in his chest and he felt as if everything was collapsing around him, but of course it wasn't. Guilt wracked through his body and the pain in his leg seemed to be a figment of his imagine as he gritted his teeth and hauled both him and the young man up. With the body in his arms Tim breathed harshly but deep sucking in the air he had and he relished the pain in his leg. He welcomed it. He wanted it, it reminded him that he had sworn to be there for his nephew but he hadn't. Christopher was lying almost dead in his arms and he hadn't even been able to see him until he had taken the time to focus properly. He had not done right by his brother and now he felt that every wound inflicted on his body hurt, ached, stung and gnawed deep to punish him. To show him that he had been a liability when he promised loyalty. Only once before had he felt this kind of rage, this kind of fear and sadness and panic.

Only once had he felt the change approaching him with such a force he wanted to drop down to his knees in order to change but he couldn't change, not with his nephew in his hands. He snarled with wolf vocal chords and howled into the night in utter fury. His felt his muscles bulking up more and he the muscles of his legs bulged. He remembered the teachings that Aliysha had been given, he had to master than now. It was not good if he changed completely, he had a life in his hands. Breathing out calmly he accepted the power while at the same he tensed his muscles and pulled his stomach in to contract the change at the same time and so remain in a half/half state. He looked over to where the Cicatrices were but couldn't see them. All he had in mind now was getting Christopher to the door; then he would unleash his fury.

The door was quite simple he saw wolves in the way of it, he saw women wolves fighting back, their thinner bodies able to move faster, their agility much better than his own and he saw Tendra… who was already looking in his arms at her son. It was terrible to see his sister turn back to human form and almost fall to her knees in grief. It was heart breaking to see her running over to him and the females all around trying hard to fight the enemy wolves so she had a clear path. He walked over to her and was almost tipped over when she dragged her son from his arms and sank to the ground with Christopher draping over her knees.

"My son. My little boy. Christopher, Christopher wake up, please wake up. Tim he won't open his eyes!"

"He isn't dead, get him in the nursery, I'll find Solomon, he patched me up when I was injured."

"Christopher. Christopher, Tim's getting help, hold on, please hold on."

Still Christopher didn't open his eyes and remained limp on the floor. When a tear slid off the side of Tendra's face Tim finally burst his control. Just like he had when he was seven he let the whole change take over him. Fur burst from his body and he was hurled to the floor with the extreme force of the change. Barking loudly, gruffly, he looked back at the smoke he had come from and towards the gates. The wayward pack were still swarming in through them. He had to find one particular wolf in the utter chaos. He looked back at Christopher. He had once promised his life to his nephew, he would keep that promise now. He ran off into the evening, towards the enemy and submerged himself in the middle of their wolf forms and their weapons of torture.

Chapter 20

Rage was a funny thing. Majestic he stood tall for a full minute with his head raised, not to howl but to scan the battleground. He needed to spot his allies and avoid them because he was about to lose control any second. For the third time now a whip had landed harshly on his back and he had refrained from letting lose a single sound. He was tensed and in perfect control and with infinite dignity he turned around in a circle to observe the enemy that were all gathered around him; watching and waiting for him to make a move. They wanted to taunt him for a while. He wasn't even sure if they wanted him dead, for sure he knew he would make a good test subject for breeding.

He couldn't observe all day though and as a stone hit the tip of his ear he snarled once and lunged forward. His claws unsheathed and he displayed them proudly before pushing them down in to the shoulders of the wolf infront of him. His own lunge took him to the floor, cushioned by the enemy though, he continued only to drag his claws through the flesh and lean down to bite at its neck; subduing it by raking his back legs down the belly of the fallen wolf underneath him.

Wolves all around him pounced and he felt their teeth but not the pain. He was so furious at the turn of events with Christopher going missing. Why did he have to turn up half dead on the battle field? Tim felt his heart in his mouth; he should have checked, he should have had Tommy scout for him. He should have double checked every single inch of the compound looking for his nephew... but no. He had been so preoccupied that his nephew didn't like him anymore that he had, instead, compromised Christopher's safety. He felt the teeth biting his legs but he bore, took it without flinching and instead kicked back. Three wolves tried to pin him but the adrenaline pumping into his muscle kept him strong. It kept his mind constantly on alert and he held his ground, pushed back and went directly for the heart whenever a wolf came near him. He may have been outnumbered but he was ferocious!

At the back of the buildings Aliysha was witness to one of his men falling. There was no bending of the legs when his man fell either; it was a stunned fall and the harsh impact was cringing. Aliysha wanted to look away but he owed his pack member more than a cowardly glance in another direction. He owed them his help but at that moment he was struggling. Overcome with wolves all running and hitting into his legs, like a stone pillars used to ram against a locked door, they were trying to tip him. They beat him with whips and sticks and threw stones. His legs were riddled now with bullet holes. He knew that at any moment he too would fall, just like the wolf from his pack. His thick muscles and large statue only helped so much and right at that moment he felt as if it simply wasn't enough.

The wolves all around him were smirking, his little pack of specialised wolves had no way to call for help or back up. At the back of everything their role was to be a surprise and they had been... for the first half hour anyway, until it had become common knowledge that their mutated selves were hiding in wait. Then they had been surrounded and as far as Aliysha could see every other wolf out on the stoned compound was also outnumber. If he called for help it would be pointless and maybe even selfish, everyone was under extreme threat and he couldn't expect any of them to come to his aid when they too needed aid and he wasn't able to get to them.

So this was the harsh reality of a war. Not just a battle but a full on war that was brutal, unfair and riddled with disaster. He looked around at all his men and he felt a pang of sadness wash over him. His men: he had trained them, fought with them and guided them through the world for the last couple of decades. He had come to love everyone of them and they were a strong community because of it. He had never found his mate and right at that moment he was glad, for it would hurt so much more if he knew he would be losing them at the end of this as well. In the corner of his eye he saw the familiar body of Tim. And Tim was going at it like crazy, if he didn't know better he would have thought Tim had lost it. But he did know better and he knew no matter what, Tim would keep his head. He hadn't seen Myco for a while and that worried him. Myco was one to constantly check on people and he missed not seeing his former Alpha.

The assault on his legs got worse, and worse, and he was gritting his teeth in pain as he bent down and swung for the wolves that hurt him. No matter how many he threw into the air, or crushed under his heavy arms, they were always replaced by double the number. It was a vicious chain of events. Get rid of one pain, double it. He felt his legs start to give up on him and the ground was slowly coming into better view. He wanted to close his eyes but he didn't, for the strong and simple reason that; he wasn't dead yet.

Tim felt heavy pressure on the back of his right thigh and he fell to the side. Immediately he was tackled fully to the floor and the breath was knocked out of him when the weight of a wolf came down on his back, right over his ribs while another deliberately stood on his front left paw to pin him. He tried to struggle but a whip lashed on his exposed paw, the sole, and it burnt and stung so bad he whined a little before he could stop the sound escaping his throat. He was fuming by now, so angry he was seeing the world through a red haze. He was at his most dangerous point and too dangerous to be around anyone he loved. He prayed someone would stop him before he hurt one of his own because he was a force that was hard to stop. He didn't need air in his lungs to get back up, he simply pushed up through his muscles. He was a man who had built his own house, lived alone with nothing but the goal to cultivate the best wolf he could be. Strength was no object now.

It didn't hurt him to push upwards though it did strain him, it teased the ropey sinews of his muscles and tickled them as he stretched upwards. The ligament running inside of him cracked from the pressure but he unbalanced the wolves that were laying on him. All the while he ignored the pain of his trod-on paw. He deliberately opened his mouth so saliva gathered and built up around his teeth and lips until it dribble over and slowly seeped down into his fur, matting it and mingling with the blood, sweat and mud. His eyes were pin pointed, the pupils so small it looked unnatural, alien, his vision was so focused he saw nothing but what was in front of him. To another it would have been dangerous to have such narrowed eyesight, his peripheral vision was knocked out but not to him. The point was to attack one at a time but so quick he didn't need to see anyone else.

No sooner had he unbalanced the two wolves on him, he bit the leg holding his paw, once released he tilted his head and attacked quickly; biting the neck of the same wolf. Turning swiftly he bent low and at last minute twisted so his belly was to the sky and his mouth clamped down on the underbelly of a lunging wolf. He was on his feet again in no time, his stomach muscles were honed to near perfection so that twists and turns were nothing hard. He ran one way, then the other, feigning his attack and he caught his next prey by surprise. This was the last run of the battle now, the bit that mattered, if he was going to die he would do so knowing he had put up the biggest fight he could possibly have done. He had won back the honour he had forsaken all those years ago when he turned his back on his pack. He felt, for the first time like he was a warrior to be proud of... A wolf worthy of its fur coat. He was Tim and he wasn't afraid anymore.

Beat. Beat. Beat beat. Beat. Beat. Beat. Beat beat.

Left, right. Left, right. Left, right. And again.

From the smoky compound that everyone thought to be their death beds came the sound of drums and footsteps and not just any footsteps either but the heavy tread of booted feet marching. Tim stopped, the red haze disappeared abruptly halted by the confusion, thankfully everyone else had stopped as well. The shooting stopped, the attacking stopped and there was no need for defending. A state of surprise and anticipation had taken over. At least this waiting put off his death, Tim thought as he watched for the feet to approach.

For a while no one came out of the trees or even entered the stony grounds... but when they did, Tim's jaw dropped. Soldiers, human soldiers walked steadily up to the broken gates and stepped over the dead. Clad in combat trousers, simple tunics and polished heavy, laced boots were a regiment whose colours or symbol he did not recognise. But the people he did recognise.

Leading the troops were the wolves that Tommy had sent out, he was ever full of resources and right now even Tim was impressed at the number of disciplined men that carried on walking onto the property.

"Told you, you did well Tim." A wolf who had changed back to human form yelled to him. One of Tommy's lads he was and he was grinning at Tim as if they were best friends. "Tommy hunted down the Rogues you helped and allowed to walk away. These are the men who did not join the people at the waterfall. He created an army especially for you Tim, though, they didn't need too much convincing. You helped quite a lot in your ten years, created a lot of supporters you never realised you had gained. This is the product of your actions Tim, this is why we are loyal to you. Finish this war Tim; you have a pack to rule. "

The soldiers walked on forward perfectly at peace with their human strength and limitations but Tim soon understood that they were no less weak because of their forms. They grabbed the weapons of the enemy and they turned it to their favour. They Did not carry guns, or weapons themselves but they used hand to hand conduct to duck and kick and punch their way out. They disarmed their opponents and they pinned them to the floor. They touched the shoulder of a wolf and dug in deep to that cluster of nerves sending them to the ground, unconscious and no threat. Tim couldn't believe his eyes. Human fighting in a what humans would call a mythical realm. And it worked.

They advanced and did not break rank even as they fought their opponents. They took on the roman style, the one of fighting the person who attacked the soldier on their right – so they were always defending their comrade in arms and trusting that their friend besides them would do the same for them. It was a good strategy; it meant they fought valiantly to save a friend, but just as hard as they expected to fight for their own lives. And it meant they never gave up; wounded soldiers sometimes give in to the pain and let death take them but Tim saw that this wasn't the case. It wasn't their life they were deciding on, it was the life of a dear friend, a wolf just like them, so they never gave up fighting, even it meant they crawled on their human knees to bring down one more opponent. They were honourable men and Tim only wished he could watch them more. But alas, he was still in the middle of a battle himself so he turned his attention back to his own threat and prepared to do his part in ending this battle.

CHapTer 21

Even Tim had to say that in the end there was little to tell. The minute the soldiers came they used a combination of martial arts and hand to hand combat to knock out most of the wayward pack. Those down but not dead were tied up and sat in the corner - to awake as prisoners whose fates would be decided at a later date.

What there was a lot to tell about however was the devastation that befell his eyes after everything had ended. Afterwards it was like the world had slowly come to a stand still. Everything seemed to move that little bit slower. Everyone was on auto pilot checking for the dead and laying them gently to one side. The wounded were hastily hurried inside what was left of the buildings but they had needed to have been first checked to ensure they were safe to go in. A lot of buildings were too unstable to be used but a few were salvageable enough to make a temporary medical base. And that was only the start of the problems. They only had field medics, those trained in emergency situations and used to using little or no medication and equipment. Doctors were needed straight away but Tim still had no idea where to get actual doctors from. Humans ones were out of the question as he would expose their entire race and that could be devastating. He hadn't really thought about the aftermath that much, hell, he hadn't want a battle in the first place let alone thought they could live through it. Besides, he had always had in mind that there were fully trained emergency medics but on hearing the cries of pain and seeing the amount of blood that one person could bleed out, he realised he had made a very, very, serious mistake.

"Ray!" he called out aloud. "Ray, we need doctors, do you know of any we can send for?!"

Ray lifted his head and looked over at Tim, "I already have some waiting. In the far building I stored a box of fireworks, set them off. I sent ahead requesting aid if it was needed and safe for them. They're doctors, for survival reasons they aren't allowed in battle, the fireworks will be a message that it's safe for them."

Tim hurried off to see if he could move the debris enough to find this single box that contained their lifeline, while acutely aware that time was running out for the seriously wounded. He hoped the medics had enough training and equipment to do something for now.

The Cicatrices were dotted about turning slowly back to their fully human forms. Many weren't turning back though, it seemed to be difficult for their bodies to accept the level of damage done to them when they were reduced in size. The wounds that were nothing on their giant sized frames were suddenly gaping holes in their human ones and they were losing too much blood for a normal person to cope with. So most stayed as a hybrid and those that were able to walk were helping to pick up the heavy pieces that had once made up the houses and homes and even compound itself. They carried the wounded to the temporary bay and tried to be as helpful as they could. The Cicatrices had proved to be incredibly useful but it was sad to see such large forms crumpled on the floor. There were those who had not made it. Their legs were mangled and while a couple yelled out that it would be alright and they would heal in time, Tim saw past their reassurances. His eyes lingered on the dead and badly wounded knowing their legs would never heal and their astonishing bodies would end up hidden under the dirt when they was all over.

Ray found Tendra unconscious, her body draped over Christopher, it seemed she had been trying to protect him. Tim had for one second felt his heart stop in his chest; it was as if he felt his very blood freeze in his veins with no pump to shoot it along his tissues. He had waited anxiously for Ray to tell him it was alright, and the surge of blood that shot along to his fingertips when Ray turned around and nodded, to Tim was a little painful but fully welcome. She had a pulse so she was not dead.

Infection festered quickly in such dirty conditions and they hurried about cleaning as best as they could but they needed to tidy up first and that only caused more dust and debris to fall everywhere. The gravel was covered in blood and wolves back in human form were already trying hard to hose it down but it didn't help so they began digging up the stones, shovelling them into a single heap so that they might replace as soon as they could. Inside overturned tables were righted. Slashed, broken, smashed and cracked wreckage was thrown out. Surfaces were bleached, floors were cleaned. Curtains and bed sheets were stripped and the ripped mattresses were put on a bonfire outside. Everyone who wasn't seriously wounded was trying to make a hospital out of complete mess and it was only creating more chaos.

All this time and Tim had not seen Tommy at all. He prayed his plotting friend had gone away somewhere in order to bring back more help for this situation as well but he knew that even thinking that meant he was becoming complacent with his secret helper.

He set off the fireworks and then searched around for his cunning friend hoping against all hope he had not fallen.

"Tommy! Tommy!" He cried. "Thomas! Don't you play any more games with me, come out now!" He swiped at a piece of metal gate that was in his way and kick at the heap of fallen bricks. His eyes were narrowed as he looked frantically around. "Tommy!"

"Over here." Someone yelled to Tim, he hurried over and stopped dead in his tracks at what he saw.

On his knees, leaning over the mangled figure of a familiar man, was Tommy... and he was holding Myco's body. "I couldn't save him Tim. I swear to you that I tried."

"It's alright... Call for Lebon." Tim ordered a wolf at his side.

Lebon was scouted out immediately and brought to the scene. "What has happened?" He asked Tim who was still shocked and looking at the rocking and distressed Tommy. He had never seen his friend like this and it was hard to watch.

"Tommy tried to save Myco but he died. Go to him Lebon, he needs his alpha now."

It was with a grave sorrow that Tim closed his eyes and left Tommy alone with the only one who could help him now. An alpha had a bond no one else did and in the midst of despair that was an alpha's duty; to pull their members back to the light. That was why a crazed alpha was so terrible, not only did he forsake his pack but no one could help him and he was lost completely.

"Tommy." Tim heard Lebon say. "Tommy let us move away now, there are many dead here. Our kin are in pieces and we need to help them. Come on Tommy, you did what you could."

"It wasn't enough. I saw him taken down... I ran to him but they... they piled on top, I killed five but it was too late. It was too late Alpha."

"Tommy, you have seen much death, you sent your - our - own men out, knowing how dangerous that was."

"But not Myco!"

"Tommy, you barely knew Myco."

"I knew him... I stayed away a lot of the time to avoid him. I took on other responsibilities because I couldn't bear to be around him."

"Tommy?"

Tim stopped in his tracks, listening. "We loved each other but we were not each other's mate. He found his mate... I couldn't be around him when I knew."

"Where is the female?"

"I took her to safety before the battle, I told Myco not to worry about her; she is already with Eveliina. I loved him enough that I never wanted to see him in pain... so I saved the one thing he loved."

But Myco was not you mate?"

"It doesn't mean I can not love, Alpha! It doesn't mean I am indifferent to everyone else. Let me alone Lebon, I'm begging you. I need to grieve."

Tim bowed his head and walked on. He demanded that no one would go near Tommy so his friend could have his request, for now. Lebon soon followed, the alpha had the look of a father in his eyes - an upset father who knew he couldn't help his child at that moment.

The doctors came, all at once they arrived and Tim could see that they had been all ready isnd awaiting the signal. He greeted them as friendly as he could but the situation was getting dire and he was urgent in his welcome.

"I'm sorry; the worse are just through here, it was the best we could make it. This is the cleanest we could do in such a short space of time."

They weren't impressed at the makeshift 'wards' but they administered what drugs they were able and got started straight away on tending to the wounded.

"Is there nowhere else that is cleaner? Somewhere safer than these buildings? It's a health hazard even being here!" One female doctor yelled at him, clearly at her wits end and when some dust fell from the ceiling she hunched over her patients leg to keep it as clean as possible.

"Outside is a mess."

"Is there anywhere else we can take them? Are there any other packs that will take you in?!"

"Have you seen how many of us there are?" Tim argued back. "What pack would take all of us in? And besides, our friends are here, they've been pulled in from far and wide for this battle, there is nowhere and no one else."

"There is somewhere."

The doors burst open but the person who spoke did not make an entrance worthy of great attention. His despondent tone of voice however did. He sounded hollow, expressionless but he was coherent and that was all that mattered. "Tim lives near a waterfall. Getting them down the rocks will be the hard bit but we can set tents up around the top of it. There's a fresh water supply and with the wayward pack all here, it's the safest we are going to get. It's the cleanest environment around and is a little away from a forest. For wolves it really is a serene place. Once they are out of danger we can get them into the caves, it offers shelter and Tim's pack already have cleaned it out. That's the best we can hope for."

The doctor took a look around at the broken cupboards and the beds with no sheets adorned on them. She took in the walls that were half crumbled and the dust that was laying around despite the constant cleaning that had been going for a couple of hours now.

"It's the best we have. Let's prepare for transfer. I'll ring a few friends and see if we can't get some vehicles to lend for the transfer."

"Tim owns a garage, there are three cars still in there - we can hot wire them and tomorrow we'll take them back and repair the wires so they're good as new for the owners."

Tommy was bent over the nearest patient to him, helping to dress his injuries and already preparing him for transfer. "I have medic skills, you can use me." He muttered away while he went about snapping up bandages and assessing yet another patient. All the while Tim was stood around a little stunned that his pack home and his business were being offered up as service by some-one other than himself but he had no intention of objecting.

"It will be cramped when we get there." He said.

"We'll take care of details once we've save everyone's life." Tommy said throwing a medical bag at Tim. "Carry that and come on."

He wanted to ask about Myco but Tommy wouldn't look at him and he seemed to be going at a high speed in order to keep his mind occupied to its fullest capacity. "Tommy?" He tried. He had to.

"Don't Tim. I know you heard but just leave it now. There are some things you don't understand and hopefully never will. I'll find my mate one day and the pain of this will fade."

"And until then?"

"I'll do what I do best. I get things done, so come on Tim! Move it!"

Not even the wolf instinct inside of him snarled at the command by someone other than an alpha of equal ranking, and secretly he smiled. He had full and utter control of his wolf again and better still – his wolf knew compassion. The orders given in grief were not a disrespect, they were a cry for help and he thanked his instincts that inside of himself he knew the difference. He hurried out running through the people and inspecting the crowd. He looked for those that were walking wounded and could get themselves to the waterfall under their own steam. He assessed who the strong and able ones were so they might help others and he noted particularly the seriously injured that needed all the aid they could get.

He himself wanted to run over to Christopher and check on him, he wanted to make sure Tendra had come around but he knew he had to think logically. They were being seen to and in order for them to have the best treatment, there had to be a place they could go to in order for the most sterile place to benefit them. Distance right now was best. It didn't help his guilt for leaving but it did make him more determined to keep up with Tommy's pace.

Who would have thought the waterfall would become a beacon for everyone he had ever known? "Aliysha!" He called out. "Have word sent to Eveliina that the battle is over, I am all right but we need them back at the waterfall straight away, and we need the able bodied to help the injured."

"Will do Tim... Marcus!"

Word rang out of relocation and soon everyone was making their way. Someone came up in the three cars from his garage, he had completely forgotten them in the hassle that had followed his boss's death and soon there were 'vans' picking up the unconscious. They couldn't be conspicuous but Tim saw inside the vans and was surprised at the layout. The back was spacious enough for a bed and there were shelves all around just like an ambulance but a little smaller.

"We don't do to badly for 'under the radar'." One of the doctors smirked at him and he nodded.

"Very true, remind me to keep in touch with you!"

"Haha, of course Alpha, Tim. I'll patch you all up any time as long you know I charge double for the cheeky ones and that includes you!"

Six hours later Eveliina was back at the waterfall, relieved and now exhausted from her travelling and the frantic rushing around she had done; boiling water, fetching and carrying, finding clothes, bed sheets, blankets and foods from their stores they had originally had to abandon. She had made the introductions as best and as quickly as she was able to when everyone had been thrown together and she spent her time running from one area to the other and taking orders from everyone. She had to find more bandages and keep the water going around. She made three trips to the shop for more supplies such as bedding and clothes and even tents at one point. She was getting used to running at a wolves pace, she had needed to adapt quickly to keep up with the heavy demands. Everyone was working at their full speed and it felt good. She felt as if she played a vital part even if she had not fought with her own hands, she was doing something good now and it made her feel even more a part of her pack.

She was stunned to find even more members and she was sure she wouldn't remember their names, but already the bond of alpha female had made it so they were slowly sticking in her mind even when she thought she was running out of space. The surrounding land was covered in white sheets held up by poles and in every cave there were groups of people. The water flowing down the stream was very dirty but thankfully the constant current of the waterfall made sure it was regularly washed away and newer, fresher water was put in its place. The amount of blood that coloured the water was shocking to see and she felt her stomach feel a little queasy at seeing it and she knew that others would no doubt be feeling the same.

The women and children sent her way from the safe passages were all around calling for their husbands and grown children and the reuniting of families was both heart breaking and heart-warming. It hurt to see mothers cry over injured sons and wives tending to the gaping wounds of their husbands but every tear shed in those scenarios were tears of joy at being together again. Some did grieve. Some had lost family and they were silent, they were already wearing black and their diligence was matched only by their silence.

It took a long time before Tim eventually pulled her to one side and told her about Tommy.

"Don't mention it, just let him do what he wants for now and he wants to stay busy I think. He hasn't stopped yet."

"I'll give him another hour but then I'll take him something eat. I won't push him." She said, smiling at Tim. He was covered in long gashes and claws marks himself and his back was bloody. She wanted to take a minute to see to him, to tend him as he was tending to everyone else but he wouldn't hear of it. With every person that dared go near him, he was hard pressed to restrain himself from lashing out at. Eveliina saw that he was preoccupied with other things and knew there was something he wasn't telling her. She hadn't ever seen his family but from the talk she had gather that the tall lady who was wearing a deep shade of blue dress, that fell to her ankle but was split to her mid-thigh, was his sister; the one he had told her about. Tendra had looked after him as a child, and Eveliina desperately wanting to go and talk to her. But the hushed voices whenever the name 'Tendra' was mentioned told her that something had happened.

"Eveliina!" Someone shouted her name and she realised that more water was need so she scuttled off hoping to make use of herself.

"You're working hard."

A voice beside her made her jump and she turned to see the smiling Tendra looking at her. "I've seen you staring at me for a while now, I thought I might as well come and say hello while you wait for the water."

"Sorry, I didn't mean to stare, it's just... Well I'm Tim's mate and I thought I should introduce myself but you look... like something is wrong."

"And everyone is being quiet around me." Tendra laughed at the sweet girl in front of her trying to be so tactful when the situation needed to be more to the point. "My son Christopher decided not to run today, he was going to show his uncle Tim that he didn't need protecting. He got jumped from behind the minute he came out of the safe passage. He defended it well against those who tried to get down it to the non-fighters but he only managed to make it outside before his wounds got the better of him."

"Oh my, I'm so sorry, I didn't-;"

"It's ok. Everyone knows, you might as well know too. Just a word of warning; Tim won't let you go near him until he knows Christopher is alright. It's his trait, he feels responsible because he didn't protect his nephew, so as his punishment to himself he won't allow himself to be treated until he knows the ones he loves are alright. He did the same when our father hurt us. He made sure if he hid under his bed or I saved him from a bad beating then he won't let me near him until I had taken care of myself first."

"He regrets leaving you, all of you. He cried when he told me he considered it to be betrayal when he left the pack but he felt suffocated. He feels selfish for pursuing his own way in life." Eveliina felt desperate to at least try and back his side.

"He shouldn't feel guilty. I know that he had to find his own way in life, Ray knows that, half our packs even knows that but Tim doesn't. The other half don't as well but he proved himself out there today so I think all can be forgotten now. Not everyone has to like the course of action one choses."

"Are you hurt?"

Eveliina noted that Tendra was favouring her right side.

"I'll be aright; I picked a few things up from Tim myself. I want to make sure Christopher is alright before I take any attention away from what could potentially be his. I had best go check on my mate; I'll let you know when Christopher is deemed alright. Then you can go to Tim."

"Welcome to the family Eveliina – I've been staring at you as well, hoping for an introduction."

Tendra walked off and left Eveliina with the hot water and a bit more knowledge and confidence than she had before. Things could only get better from now on; already she looked around at the waterfall that was so alive with activity. Yes there had been deaths and funerals to arrange but looking at the pack all settled in and the many packs all allied together with wolves from all over coming to help each other she smiled. She could never have imaged this in a million years and certainly not after her own pack was destroyed. But here it was, that peaceful world she had always dreamt a part of.

"Eveliina!"

But not just yet, the peace would come when she got to sleep in the day after...

EPILOGUE

He was frustrated with everything. The pack he had brought together for Tim was going perfectly; they got on, and they were building a bloody fortress by the waterfall. Ray, Lebon and Aliysha (in his mutated form), where rebuilding the safe house and adding underground links to and from the waterfall. They ate dinner together every night and Tim was even building that garage business up while trying to attend to the needs of his pack and his mate and his family. Christopher was fighting fit – well he was walking with crutches and he had finally forgiven Tim. It would take a while for him to trust Tim as inexplicably as he used to as a child but that was to be expected, Tim was just glad that Christopher was filling him in about all the years they had lost out on and would eat dinner alongside of him. But for Tommy he was frustrated because his happy ending wasn't as simple.

It had been hard enough to acknowledge to himself that he was gay. He didn't want to tell his pack mates in case they thought worse of him, turns out they didn't but they were surprised. He could deal with that, he could deal with the label but what he couldn't deal with was that he lost the one person he loved. He had spent ages convincing 'Natalia' to go into safety while Myco was fighting and he had only done that to please Myco. He loved him and he wasn't around anymore. It felt as if the trouble he had gone to meant nothing. Even thought he had saved a woman's life, it still didn't seem enough. It felt as if a piece was missing from inside of him.

He looked around at the happy people, the merging packs and the many toasts in the name of peace amongst each other's protection and security. And he couldn't join in; it was as if he didn't belong in the happiness. So he had decided to leave for a while, to go and get his head in gear again then return all positive and quirky as he used to be.

"You know you walk a little crouched, do you have a medical condition?"

"Do you want a medical condition? I can give you one if you ask a question like that again!" Tommy replied angrily.

He turned around to the rude person who was analysing his 'gait' as he liked to call it.

"Wow, wow I didn't mean any offense. Were you hurt in the fighting? I noticed you didn't come by to any of the doctors to be checked out afterwards."

"I don't need a doctor."

"Let me make sure."

He hadn't fully looked at the man before but he was now; who on earth was being as forward as this.

"I mean I couldn't help but notice you around camp, and you always disappear, I lose track of you a lot but I know you didn't come to the medical tents to be seen."

"Who are you?"

"My name is Andrai, I'm a doctor."

Tommy looked at him and then he felt... different. It was as if he needed to go over there and let the doctor check him over.

Hell that sounded really good... but he was grieving! He was upset; he felt loss at the thought of Myco. So why was this new feeling sliding up alongside the grief and slowly trying to overtake it? Well, maybe push it away somehow but not take it away. It was trying to cohabit with the grief, this new, strange, feeling.

"I don't care who you are I don't need anyone now leave me alone."

"Please I'm worried about you."

"Why?"

Don't say it, don't say it, don't say it. The same three words rang in his head while he closed his eyes and had his back to the new stranger.

"Grief is hard, I know it is, but you do get through it. You really do need your arm seeing to, I know you're injured there at the very least. Just let me help you, let me be a doctor and then you can do what you want and I won't get in the way."

Tommy didn't understand, he wanted to turn around and take the man up on his offer but it felt like a betrayal to Myco. "Come on, let me take the physical pain away even if I can't take the emotional pain away." This strange man was still chatting on! But that was the problem because Tommy felt caught up in headlights; the guy was taking the emotional pain. At least, he was dulling it a little.

"We'll take it as slow as you want Tommy, you can't deny what we are to each other, you know you can't. So I'll let you grieve as long as you need but I need to take care of you. Come to me Tommy."

He had no choice, the voice was calling him and he walked over to the strange man who wrapped his arm around him and held him tightly; held him dearly and took away the cold that had settled into his bones when the grief came. He couldn't understand why now, why the bad timing but as he felt slowly warmer and safer and not as alone, he started to think that maybe this was the perfect time.

"Andrai, you're my mate."

www.ingramcontent.com/pod-product-compliance
Lightning Source LLC
Chambersburg PA
CBHW070958190726
48292CB00004B/1500